Something in the Water

A Superior Murder Mystery

by Mike Savage

First Edition

Second Printing, September, 1998

© Copyright 1998 Michael P. Savage

Cover Illustration ©1998 Stephen Staurseth

ISBN 1-886028-32-X

Library of Congress Catalog Card Number: 98-065200

Printed in the U.S.A.

DEDICATION/ACKNOWLEDGMENTS

This book is dedicated to my Ma, Elsie Greener. She is the epitome of strength. She describes herself as, "one tough old broad." She taught me to, "take 'er as she comes," and "let the tail go with the hide."

Thanks Tish, for mongo typing, talking and listening. Thanks Bob, for all the great lunches and steady friendship. Thanks Mary, for asking all the right questions. Thanks Beth, for pointing out that there are many types of books in me. Thanks Snowflake, for taking me fishing. Thanks Georgeann, for always being on fast forward. Thanks Phoebe, for being a great sister and an exceptionally good reader/reflector. Thanks Teddy, for sharing insights and reading with sharp attention for detail. Thanks to Diane, the low-life Anchor Queen, for great proof reading. Thanks Anna, for excellent reading and your hard work in the publishing quarry. Thanks John, for proofing and commenting.

PROLOGUE

In the late 1950's and early 60's over two thousand 55-gallon drums were dumped in Lake Superior. These barrels have periodically tickled the media's fancy and continue to fascinate a few "environmentalists" who can't stand to let a sleeping dog tell falsehoods. During the last feeding frenzy when some barrels were raised and found to contain just what was said to be in them, my friend Judi and I started joking around about what "could" be in those barrels. This story just goes to show what can happen when two basically unstable people fail to curtail their imaginations.

1

Alphonse "Dave" Davecki stuck a long, greasy french fry in his mouth. His face spread into a wholesale smile while his jaw kept busy chewing. Davecki didn't normally smile. He was a cop. He was a detective on the Superior force. "Detective Dave" some people called him. Right now though, he was just another satisfied customer in the Anchor Bar enjoying Ruthie's raw fries and the finest mushroom and swiss hamburger in five states. Davecki picked up his bottle of root beer and tipped the sasparilla in with the fry. He was enjoying this as much as any cop can enjoy food —or anything for that matter. He'd need the small pleasure in the days to come, for, little did Davecki know, a mere six miles away, on one of the most beautiful beaches in the world, Thurber Gronsby was washing ashore as a dead man.

In the meantime, Davecki continued to enjoy the Anchor. It was far and away the funkiest bar in the Twin Ports. Tom had the joint jammed floor to ceiling with nautical crap of every kind. Bean provided the one ingredient essential to all successful recipes, spice with a capital "S." Ruthie made burger magic happen over and over again on her hot grill in the corner. Sneering college kids from Duluth mingled with the yuppie-types from Minnesota Power who rubbed shoulders with welders from Barko Hydraulics where heavy equipment for the logging industry was built. Low-life drunks nursed precious bottles across the table from chug-a-lug poets who spilled their beer and crack-pot philosophies on whomever would listen. Usually their victims were defenseless doctors and lawyers trying to recapture their days as shiftless students. A lot of the docs were from SMDC, the hospital that resulted from the merger of Saint Mary's and the Duluth Clinic. They usually showed up at the Anchor with their lawyer friends who teased them saying, "All you guys accomplished was to make the **S**ame **M**edicine at **D**ouble the **C**ost."

In other words, the Anchor was a dive. The perfect place to dive in and be real. Davecki wasn't so much a cop in the Anchor as he was just another hungry, thirsty schmuck who needed what the Anchor offered —good cheap food in an unpretentious atmosphere where nobody in the entire joint gave two hoots for who, or what, you were. Not once in twenty years of stopping for fries and beer had Davecki ever heard a cell phone ring. Not once had a beeper gone off. In fact, he'd never actually seen Bean cup her hand over the phone and shout out someone's name. That was one reason Davecki liked the Anchor. He could sit in the big old barber chairs, swivel forth and back looking at the pool players, the theater students smoking too much and the make-out artists in the corner.

He could be reassured by the dingy flag of the Great Lakes Fleet sagging sadly from the ceiling. He could stare down artifacts he'd never really seen in two decades of visits. He could sit in peace and feast his eyes on old block and tackle, ship's clocks, time cards, photos of vessels at anchor, photos of vessels before they sank, photos of vessels *after* they sank, photos of ships with record loads of iron ore forcing them low in the water. His eyes could seek out weight slips in metric and long tons, brass pressure gauges, antique artifacts from vessels long ago cut into scrap iron and made into Toyotas. Davecki, while having to grunt the occasional "hey" to someone heading to the john who knew him from an earlier arrest, could just sit and look the joint over without worrying about anything.

He was studying a section of wall he'd examined often. There were the photos of the storm tossed ore boat with its deck completely awash in waves. He'd seen the brass porthole ring hundreds of times. He'd studied the dusty bos'on's knot before, tracing its twists and turns. He'd seen the mannequin with her nipple-less boobs, the stuffed swordfish, the old Jitterbug fishing lure and the picture of the Stmr. John A. Simenson in dry dock at Fraser shipyards just down the waterfront a mile. But still, Davecki knew there had to be something on that wall he'd never seen. The Anchor was like those magic eye things in the Sunday edition of the *Duluth Snooze Tribune*. Tom always added new junk to the Anchor walls, ceilings and floors, and it always hid out in embarrassment amongst the rest of the seafaring flotsam.

Concentrating on the walls and enjoying his last mouthful of food, it took Davecki a second to realize something very unusual was going on in the bar. People were looking at him. Bean was holding a bottle of Absolut in mid-pour. The chick with the chest who had been trying for a half an hour to get Davecki to look at her was just standing at the back end of the table holding her stick. The thought of his stick in those capable looking hands crossed Davecki's mind. But it would never be, for his right brain was demanding that he pay attention to whatever it was that had put the entire Anchor Bar on hold.

He snapped out of his daydream and started clawing at the opening to his brown bomber jacket. He was embarrassed and ashamed. His cell phone was ringing. He'd forgotten to shut the damn thing off when he entered and now, after decades of fitting in, he was breaking the unwritten law of the Anchor. He was standing out in the crowd.

Davecki got the phone out and stabbed a button. "Yeah," he said as the chick with the grip on the cue bent down to take her next shot and show her cleavage. The rest of the bar took themselves off pause as the sheepish cop listened intently to the little black tumor-maker at his ear.

Bean walked around the bar and headed for the barber chairs where Davecki was seated. The pool babe took her stroke smoothly. At least she held her cue properly, Davecki observed. The balls clacked together and Davecki spotted the new artifact on the wall. It was a brass nameplate that said "Alarm Bells" peeking out from behind the baggage cart. But he didn't care anymore. What he heard changed his day and, really, his life. Bean walked up and said, "Shut that damn thing off and enjoy yourself, Davecki."

"Yeah, sure," Davecki said lowering the phone and stabbing "end." His slender face had lost its mirth.

The darkness of his Chippewa-tinted skin had gone white. The normal lively dance of his pale blue, deep-set eyes was gone. His shoulders sagged.

"What's the problem?" Bean asked, seeing her patron was shaken.

Davecki stuffed the phone in his pocket. He was looking directly at the busty pool babe as she approached and extended her right hand.

"I'm Dizzy Derquist," she said.

Davecki didn't take her hand. He hadn't really heard her. He had barely heard Bean's question, though he answered automatically as he got out of the swivel chair and took off for the door, "Thurber Gronsby is dead."

2

Somewhere between the North End and when he turned left on Moccasin Mike Road, Davecki realized he'd screwed up by telling Bean about Gronsby.

The dazed detective shook his head and pushed the Mustang's accelerator pedal to the floor. Davecki always drove Mustangs. He always went to Saturday evening Mass, and he always drove too fast. Luckily he was a cop. He had an excuse most of the time. But, there was something mundane about high speed runs like this one. With a flashing Kojak perched on top of the roof people knew he was a cop. Sometimes a downright thrill ride was the only thing that fulfilled his need for speed. On those occasions Davecki gave himself a fix in any number of ways. His favorite was the official **Dave Davecki-Anchor Run.**

Created and administered by Hizonner Himself, Alphonse Dave Davecki, the Anchor Run was nine point three miles (give or take a tenth depending on the route chosen) from the Anchor to the Anchor via the two bay bridges. His best time ever was on his '87 Honda Magna. The original rules stated that the participant (himself) had to start the stop watch, drink a full glass of tap beer, slam a shot of whiskey and leave the bar with no sign of haste. It was unlawful to attract attention by rushing out.

But once outside, all the rules ended. The object was to get going and get back without getting caught speeding. Basic decorum was out. Even road rage was permissable, if it was necessary. But usually anger was superfluous at a hundred and thirty miles an hour.

Decorum was the rule again upon re-entry into the Anchor. The stopwatch stopped when his ass found a seat. The sentence was nine point three miles at speed beginning with a calm capital and ending with an equally calm period. It was 48,576 feet of frenzy punctuated with two leisurely hundred foot strolls.

His best time ever was seven minutes and forty-two seconds. It was invigorating, that trip. It was a strange satisfaction to walk into the bar calmly his heart beating wildly from the adrenalin. There was some sort of evil glee that rose within him as he eased into the barber chair knowing that he'd just stepped out for a few minutes to average 105.14 miles-an-hour, been to another state and an altered state.

Such foolishness was completely unjustified of course, but it was fun. Those days were long gone. Now Davecki had a reason to speed.

This early evening in June, the Mustang's leap to eighty miles an hour was excusable. Thurber Gronsby, Bonnie the dispatcher had said, was dead. Davecki tightened his large, long fingered hands on the "Stang's" black leather-wrapped steering wheel. Those hands were connected to a rather average body. At five foot eleven and two hundred pounds, Davecki wouldn't be winning any major bar fights. But one time, he'd wrestled with a pet Vietnamese pig that went two twenty five if it weighed a pound. The owner of said animal decided it would be, "interesting to watch" if he fed his swine some meth. The downstairs neighbors called the cops to the duplex at 2015

Something in the Water

Baxter Avenue, because they thought the house was falling down. The young cop impressed everyone by impulsively tackling the crazed creature and hog tying it with an extension cord from the lava lamp.

Davecki automatically turned his left turn signal on before he realized he'd made yet another mistake. The crime scene wasn't at the near end of the Point. It was past the dump, out at Dutchman's Creek, the place the Finns called Bare-Ass Beach.

Davecki flicked the lever back and sped past the dump on his right. Hundreds of seagulls circled overhead like vultures in a western movie scene. The car jumped off the blacktop. Flying rocks hit the bottom of his beloved Mustang like exploding popcorn hitting the pot's lid. He lifted his right foot. The white and black trimmed car slowed remarkably fast. Davecki had torn down and rebuilt the engine to his own demanding performance specifications which included high compression pistons, roller bearing rockers, Boss valves and a long duration cam. The mill was especially good at engine braking. The rear wheels skidded to the left a little. Davecki counter-steered, correcting the slide.

As the car slowed to a reasonable speed for the ruts on the gravel and clay-surfaced road, Davecki rubbed a tear out of his left eye. "Damn dust," he muttered knowing fully that the Stang was as well insulated against such infusions as the driver was against admissions of emotional involvement with a case. This case was going to be different. Thurber Gronsby was universally loved and admired by everyone in town. Since retiring from the force, he'd endeared himself for trying to coerce someone, any-one —Honeywell, the government— to clean up Lake Superior by removing the mysterious barrels on the lake's bottom. Now Gronsby was found dead on Wisconsin Point.

Wisconsin Point is, for two months —three on a good year— one of the most beautiful beaches in the world. Eight miles of sand from the Wisconsin entry with its huge red-roofed lighthouse to the impassable red clay banks to the east, the Point was a fairly popu-lar picnic spot for families, a more popular spot for make-out fests and most popular for underage drink-ing at bonfire illuminated beer bashes. The keggers took place mostly on the near end, Davecki knew. As a young patrolman he'd broken up many a party, trans-ported many a thirteen-year-old girl who was too drunk to realize her sweatshirt was on backwards and that her bra strap was hanging out of her blouse's arm hole. He couldn't count the number of times a drunk kid had thrown up in the back seat of his squad. It was a good thing the Point was buried under sixteen feet of snow and ice for six or eight months of the year. Everyone knew Gronsby loved Wisconsin Point. He'd held press conferences out there. He'd written editorial pieces from, "The Point." He'd submitted photos of driftwood, waves, sunbathers and sand sculptures to the "Daily Smelly Gram."

Davecki slowed the Mustang even more. The throaty exhaust mumbled like a bar hooker's smoky voice as he shifted from fifth gear directly to third.

Something in the Water

He piloted the car around a huge washout on the right and pointed the nose downhill toward the alder-crowded marsh of Dutchman's Creek. Even though it was still as bright as noon at nine p.m., Davecki could detect faint flashes of red against the lush green foliage.

Davecki pulled up behind a white squad whose Jetsonic light bar was pulsing. Squad fourteen, he noted, and looked at the Stang's dashboard digital just below his clanging St. Christopher medal. Nine seventeen. When he looked back up, Haybales, the second-shift Commander-in-Chief of squad fourteen was walking past the black Volvo 244 station wagon that was behind the squad. As Bales approached the Stang, Davecki got out and pulled his bomber tighter. It was June twenty-first, the longest day of the year, and though the rest of the country was sweltering in a heat wave, Lake Superior, like Denali in Alaska, created its own weather. "Colder by the lake" had become a deeply ingrained phrase to the people of the Twin Ports. Zipping his jacket half-way up, Davecki said, "Hey Bales. Who called the M.E. so fast?" He nodded at the Volvo.

Officer Tommy O'Baily looked at Davecki through piercing blue eyes. His black hair and swarthy skin hinted at his Dark Irish heritage. "Can't believe he's dead," Bales said. Then, after a short pause, he added, "I did."

The men looked at each other briefly and then looked away quickly. The surrounding lush foliage was better to look at than each other's sad faces. "He's across the creek about a hundred yards," Bales said jerking his head to the left.

Davecki looked across the slough toward the lake. A strand of sand spread out from the clay bank where the turn-around ended. Fifteen yards beyond the lapping waters of Dutchman's Creek on the south were the lapping waters of Lake Superior to the north. Beyond that Davecki's eyes gorged themselves on three hundred and sixty five miles of liquid. Four quadrillion gallons. Ten percent of all the world's fresh water lay before him, and, as he walked past an eye-rubbing officer O'Baily, he felt that familiar, reassuring feeling he always felt when approaching "Da Big Lake," as the fishermen in his home town, Cornucopia, called it. "Got a suspect present?" Davecki asked.

"Nope. Anonymous phone call, Bonnie said," O'Baily replied.

"Caller I.D.?" Davecki asked rubbing his hand through his hair which was too long for his comfort. He'd need a haircut before this was over.

"Bonnie said it was a cell phone. That the guy sounded out of breath, nervous," O'Baily said. He looked past Davecki, across the marsh.

"Or scared shitless," Davecki said.

"Finding a dead body on the beach during your evening jog will do that," O'Baily said.

Davecki turned and walked toward the lake. Behind him he heard Bales say, "Damn dust." Ahead of him he saw the sand and the thin strip of Dutchman's Creek water that trickled into the lake. He knew there'd be plenty of sand in his black ankle high boots before this was over. He knew there would be wet feet from jumping unsuccessfully across the creek. He knew he'd be fighting back the urge to puke when he saw Gronsby dead. Just like he knew how he felt about Lake Superior after interviewing for a Captaincy on the Scottsdale, Arizona force. His first days in the desert were invigorating. Then he noticed his "disease." The feelings of being ill didn't go away until the drive home from Minneapolis/St. Paul airport. When he got to Esko and smelled the lake air a palpable sense of relief washed over Davecki. Then, when he crested Thompson Hill and saw the Big Lake after a week in the desert the sense of security that returned convinced him he would say no to the job offer, the pay raise, the easy winters. All so he could stay near the Great Lady, Lake Superior.

He also knew he wouldn't puke at the sight of Gronsby's body if he just kept a part of his mind focused on the huge mistress to his left. The Lake always put him in perspective, it was a good thing to live with a constant reminder of his smallness.

As Davecki threaded his way around and over the scattered driftwood, he thought about Thurber Gronsby. Gronsby had made a name for himself as an eco-warrior, a champion of the environment, particularly the Lake Superior environment. Davecki dodged a huge pile of blackened driftwood sitting in the middle of a circle of gray ashes. The bonfire remains was ringed by numerous beer bottles and cans. He considered the irony that everyone present at the beach party and bonfire who had left the bottles and cans behind probably supported Gronsby's campaign to remove the mysterious barrels of "harmless hardware" dumped in the lake by Honeywell during the late 50's and early 60's.

Davecki stopped walking toward the people standing fifty yards further down the beach. He returned to the bonfire remains and looked the scene over. A big log was pulled up beside the dead fire site. There were marshmallow roasting sticks protruding from the sand, stuck there by revelers like some weird picket fence. There had been a party recently, otherwise those sticks wouldn't be standing. Was it last night? Davecki pulled one of the sticks from the line of sentry-like saplings and prodded the extinct fire. Ash dust poofed up and swirled around like the dust devils that roamed the hardwood floors of his home. Stirring more, Davecki uncovered coals. They were still slightly glowing. The party was recent he noted with a heavy sigh. Depending on the time of Thurber's death, every single person at that party was a suspect.

"Damn," he said out loud. Davecki threw the marshmallow stick down and turned toward his final meeting with Thurber Gronsby, ex-environmentalist.

3

Thurb was dead all right. Davecki looked down at the corpse and knew his old buddy instantly. Of course he had his favorite long white coat on. He was also tightly wrapped in a gill net. He looked like a dead Siskiwit trout that had been hauled up rapidly from six fathoms. That is, his skin was bloated and ballooning out of the net's mesh squares like orderly marshmallows. A round, lamprey mark glared up from the grey flesh of his left cheek. Thurber was not only dead, he was showing his age. A large swatch of gray hair swooshed back like a Nike symbol from his temple toward his ear. The color of the gill net's cord matched the hair color perfectly because the string virtually vanished from sight where it crossed the gray. Gronsby had let his locks grow fashionably long in his last days, Davecki noted.

Gathered around the body was the medical examiner, Brian Hasaan and Officer Kevin Strum. Hasaan was from Dubai, in the United Arab Emirates. He'd taken the job as M.E. to fulfill the community service requirement attached to his medical school loans. As the Chief Detective, Davecki met Hasaan at a formal meeting between the department heads and the new M.E. The brief story Hasaan shared as a self-introduction intrigued Davecki and he invited the M.E. to that northland staple, "coffee" at Dean's Express.

"I'm a tea drinker, if that's acceptable," Hasaan said.

"Fine," answered Davecki who instantly knew he

liked the Arab. At six feet tall and weighing all of 160 pounds, there was a Scarecrow of Oz quality to the man that Davecki found haunting. Hasaan's goatee warmed up his sharp featured face, but the piercing brown eyes set deep in the olive skin of the Mideast tribes were fierce. Over tea Hasaan shared the background of his life in more detail. He was a member of the "lucky sperm club," as Davecki called rich kids. Born to a mid-level royal family in a minor emirate, the lad Hasaan went to boarding school in London about the same time the emirates, growing richer by the second as more oil discoveries were made, got together. By the time he finished his residency he couldn't return home because he'd converted to Christianity from Islam. In accordance with Shariah Law, his brother had vowed to kill Hasaan for deserting Allah.

"Any idea on T.O.D. Brian?" Davecki asked the lanky doctor.

"Who knows? Could've been a few hours ago or a day or so. Can't tell for sure, could only guess. We'll know for sure after the autopsy comes back from St. Paul," Hasaan said. The doctor pulled his heavy quilted jacket tighter around his thin shoulders. "Man, it's cold," he complained.

Davecki, in his half-opened bomber looked at Strum who stood across the body from the other two. Strum shrugged his wide shoulders which were clad in only a short sleeve blue officer's tunic which stretched tightly across his Kevlar imprisoned chest. Strum was a giant of a man. He was the Jeremiah

Something in the Water

Johnson of the Superior Police Force. He could have been an NFL lineman had he been interested in dietary steroids and incessant weight lifting. Instead he opted for a quiet life living with his school teacher wife and two kids in a log cabin the couple had built themselves. "It's the longest day of the year and certainly one of the warmest on record," Strum said looking at Hasaan.

"I'm always cold," the M.E. said. "Back home it'd be 130 right now."

"And that home would be.....Hell?" Davecki asked.

"This world is not my home," Hasaan answered with a laugh. He continued, "and if my brother ever does get his dash-dash on me I'm going to heaven, not the Hot Place."

"Lucky you," Davecki teased.

The three men stood in silence for a few seconds before Strum shifted his rugged body uneasily and said, "Bales is getting a body bag."

"Well, I suppose we'd better do a little police work." Davecki answered. "Any sign of foul play?" Davecki asked loudly.

"There was a demented-looking naked Finlander with a bloody ax fleeing into the woods," Strum answered, "But he looked normal so I didn't tackle him."

"Good," Davecki said, "One thing the Department can do without is another lawsuit."

Strum laughed. "Hey, I would never use unnecessary force!" he said putting up his hands in mock defense.

"With your bulk, a gentle caress would amount to unnecessary force," Hasaan said.

"Hey, just 'cause you're a twiggy-man sawboner, doesn't mean there isn't room for some politically correct diversity on the force. I just happen to be cholesterol challenged." Strum said.

"I never implied your impending heart attack would be anything but a much hoped for and long awaited joyous moment for us all," Hasaan said.

"I love you too, Doc," Strum said.

"Knock it off you two," Davecki commanded. They looked at the detective and both raised their eyebrows. "Okay, so you can't determine the time of death precisely, Brian. Can you estimate it? I mean, was he on the beach before or after the party around that bonfire broke up?"

"What party?" Strum asked looking around.

Hasaan swiveled his head too and then looked down at the mess below. "Who knows when he died? Could have been days ago," he said looking up and out to the Big Lake. "With this water temperature, if he drowned, it could've been days ago, or hours ago depending on how long he was submerged."

"Any sign of trauma, a blow to the head?" Davecki said squatting down to scrutinize Gronsby's nice hair.

Hasaan looked down. "Not unless you call being all wrapped up in a fishing net and sinking to the bottom of a monstrous puddle of ice water trauma," the M.E. said with a snort.

Strum chuckled too.

Davecki stood quickly and looked out across the

sparkling blue waters. Little lapping waves tickled the hard sand closest to the waterline. "That's not just a fishing net. It's a gill net and it's an old cotton one with two inch mesh. Hasn't been legal for years," Davecki said and paused. The detective looked away from the water. He looked past the two men and stared at the shimmering aspen leaves quaking on the tree-tops of the "popple" trees leaning off the top of the tall red clay bank about thirty yards away.

"Unless what?" Hasaan asked.

Davecki looked back at the blue, ice cold water. "Unless you're an Indian fisherman." he said shaking his head.

4

The three men were intent on the examination of their former friend's body and didn't notice a lone figure approaching from the east. Fortunately it wasn't a dark and stormy night, but the person approaching was walking a dog and it wasn't Snoopy.

"What's up?" a voice hailed them from down the beach.

The three men looked toward Port Wing and saw a handsome woman and a big shaggy dog.

"Official police business," Strum said turning to block the woman's approach. As the big cop turned, the scraggly black and caramel colored dog by the lady's side leapt forward and started barking.

Strum tensed and reached for his six cell MagLite. The nifty illuminators had replaced PL-22's and night sticks long ago and were hard to classify as weapons in a court of law. The big man didn't draw the flashlight from the ring on his equipment belt, but he was ready to do so in an instant.

The mace would be a better choice, Davecki thought.

The dog, it quickly became clear, wasn't interested in chomping big chunks out of Strum's ample flesh to protect it's fair mistress from the big man. It was more interested in the bundle of rotting cells in a white jacket that used to be Thurber Gronsby.

Isn't that the way it always goes? Davecki thought. Then he corrected himself. The way it always went? The dog rushed up to the corpse barking a big booming bark that came from deep within its large chest. The barks trans-mogrified into a series of growls, snarls and whines that reminded Davecki of talking.

"You probably don't want to see this ma'am," Strum said advancing on the woman. His hands were spread out low and wide like he was Davecki's grandma shooing chickens into the pen for the night.

"What?" the woman said peering around Strum's bulky body. "Just stay back, ma'am," Strum said using his command voice.

"And call your dog, damn it," Davecki shouted.

The dog was lunging forward and emitting the unusual vocalizations. The hair on the back of Davecki's neck stood up in fright as the dog summoned enough courage to nip at the netting that encased Gronsby's purple and pink hand.

"Shoo!" Hasaan screeched.

"Puddles!" The woman yelled. "Heel, Puddles!"

Davecki, fear mounting, saw that the dog's lunging had kicked up a spray of the coarse beach sand. The granules splattered across Thurb's face and landed in his permanently open brown eyes. The woman dodged Strum and grabbed the dog by the long fur on its back. Strum turned and came toward the lady. Hasaan backed away from the ruckus. The woman was yanked backwards on Puddle's fur and scolded, "Bad dog. Bad dog."

Puddles was lunging and nipping like a sled dog at the start of the Beargrease Race.

"Get away!" Davecki shouted again.

"You shut up. You're not helping," the lady screamed.

24

For some reason, Davecki expected Gronsby to blink, flinch, or reach up and try to protect his eyes from the sand. Nothing happened and Davecki saw the absoluteness of death. Something inside the detective went pop! He'd had enough of the fool dog Puddles. He reached inside his beloved bomber, unsnapped the underarm holster and pulled out his black Glock 40. "Lady, get your fucking dog away or I'll shoot it!" Davecki bellowed.

"Puddles, come Puddles," the brown haired lady shrieked. "Puddles, you bad dog," the woman scolded as Davecki looked at her and saw that she was wearing a rose-colored tank-top and that she was bra-less. This he knew because in her fight with Puddles, the tank-top wasn't topping so well.

"Heel, Puddles.... please!" the woman yelled.

Davecki holstered the Glock, circled the Gronsby artifact and landed a mighty kick square in the chest of the insane animal. The dog yelped and flinched and must have made some doggy conclusion that there was an alternative to frenzy. The dog retreated so fast that she knocked her master flat on her butt in the sand. Davecki knew the dog was a bitch for sure because a long series of bare nipples sagged below the belly of the now cringing animal. There must be little puppies somewhere.

"Hey! That's animal brutality!" The woman yelled as she flung Puddles off to her side and re-tanked her top. Puddles suddenly decided, the way dogs do, to sit down and shut up. It pulled its haunches under itself, wrapped its bushy tail around to its toes, opened its long mouth and flopped out its slimy tongue into a concentrated panting. Its eyes changed from insane-frenzy to "dum-de-dum-what'sup-doc" in a second and Davecki knew his old pal Gronsby's flesh was never really that much in danger from such an utterly stupid mutt. He wondered if dog and master were alike.

His wonder was shattered like a pane of glass by the woman's hysterical scream of, "THURBERRR!" and Davecki knew he had a suspect.

Bales came rushing up, black body bag in one hand, a video camera in the other. "What'sup?" he asked as the woman's scream darted off across the waves toward Duluth and Canada.

"Everything is under control," Davecki said. He remembered Alexander Haig.

Strum repositioned himself between the water and the body. Hasaan closed up the distance he'd put between himself and the fray. Davecki wanted to brush the sand off Gronsby's face. The woman sobbed and issued diminishing moans of "Thurber, Thurber, Thurber...."

Davecki consciously slowed his breathing. The woman, tiring of staring at the blank face of the former eco-warrior, covered her face with her own hands and further reduced her grief by turning her sobs inward.

"What'samatter with her? Bales asked.

"Found the wrong picnic," Strum said.

The woman's crying volume rose. "Knock it off," Davecki said. He ran the fingers of his right hand through his thick brown hair. His scalp was sweaty.

26

Mike Savage

Hasaan, using an obvious-to-Davecki bedside manner, said, "What's your name, ma'am?"

The woman tried to stop her sobbing. Her sides heaved. The muscles in her neck bulged. Words were crowding around in the front of her mouth like second graders crowding the door for recess. Puddles drooled.

"Just breathe ma'am," Davecki added, trying to imitate Doc Hasaan's soothing tone.

The woman drew a long breath. She took it deep. She held it a second too long and let it out too quickly. On that strained exhale she said, "Hazel. I'm Hazel Cheney." She said before breathing in again.

"I'm sorry about your dog, Hazel. I didn't mean..."

"No that's okay," Hazel interrupted. "Most of the time I hate her. It wouldn't have hurt if you'd shot her, except for the puppies."

"Hazel," Davecki started to say, but the woman looked up at him and interrupted again, "Everyone calls me Hazi."

Davecki was irked by the nickname. He counted to ten and resumed. "Hazi, you knew Thurber Gronsby?"

"Knew him?" Hazi said making moves to stand. "Knew him? Hell, we were lovers for thirteen years."

All the men looked away.

"He.... it.....that," she finally said pointing to the body as she stood up, "wasn't here an hour ago."

Instantly Davecki crossed an entire category of suspects off his list, bonfire party-goers. Maybe this case wouldn't be so hard after all he thought. He turned

27

to Bales and nodded toward the body bag. Bales put the artifact of death behind his back.

"I'll walk you down the beach aways," Davecki said to Hazi. He stretched out his arm toward the Wisconsin Entry. Hazi wobbled around Gronsby's worn looking Redwing boots as Strum stepped back to let her pass. Puddles followed her, oblivious to the Gronsby body which held such fascination moments ago. Davecki envied the dog's oblivion before following it.

"Tape the scene and bag'em," Davecki whispered to Strum as he passed. Davecki stepped around Puddles' wagging upright tail to get alongside Hazi, he heard Strum say to Bales, "Hey Bales, did'ja hear about the KKK rally in Oulu this weekend?"

"No shit," Bales said.

"Really?" Hassaan asked.

"Yeah, all them Finns are getting together for Koffee, Kake and Kookies," Strum said laughing. The last thing Davecki heard behind him was the unmistakable sound of a body bag being unfolded.

Mike Savage

5

Puddles led Davecki and Hazel up the beach. *Why was it up?* Davecki wondered. Who made the rules on such matters?

"Let's sit," Davecki said gesturing to the huge weathered white spruce log on their left. It was the same one that was used by the bonfire partiers. Silently, Hazel veered toward the natural bench. She detoured around the upright marshmallow sticks and weaved through the deep sand negotiating the shifty footing with Davecki's arm on her elbow. The sand on Wisconsin Point was different than the sand in Cornucopia. In the hot summer sun, when walking on the Corny sand, every footstep produced a barking noise. Here, the sand was as silent. Davecki knew there'd be no clues from it. Puddles went down the beach twenty yards. The dog looked back and saw the duo had stopped. Davecki watched the dog watching them. Was it thinking or was it as stupid as it looked? He sat next to his prime suspect who'd taken a seat on the rough log. Davecki was always blessed with the curse of being observant. A good trait for any cop. But it was a pain in the ass too —or, he corrected himself, in the head.

It was always like this at the crime scene, his mind racing, his thoughts demanding attention, his stream of consciousness getting longer and longer, twisting and turning like an old muddy river keep on flowing delta waters, big mama won't you come out tonight buffalo gals......

Something in the Water

"**GOD, THAT'S BEAUTIFUL!**" Davecki said. Hazel flinched. Puddles barked once. Davecki had successfully snapped his reverie by pointing out at the lake and declaring his love.

"You scared me," Hazel said.

"Sorry. It's just that I love the lake so," Davecki confessed.

"So did Thurb," the woman on his left said. "You know what I remember most about him?" she asked.

Davecki was mostly sure he didn't want to know and was certain she wasn't asking permission to share.

"He wore such lovely coats. That white one," she said nodding down the beach, "was his favorite."

Davecki knew he was doing sloppy police work. He knew someone should be present, that he should be recording this conversation. But, hell, it didn't matter. This was Superior, Wisconsin not *NYPD Blue*. Besides, he counselled himself, these crimes always solved themselves if the cops could just avoid pulling a Boulder. Poor Jon Benet, Davecki thought and he needed to divert his stream of consciousness again.

"What's the story with you two?" Davecki asked. He wondered if she had a cell phone and could imitate a man's voice.

"We met when his dad came to our farm to inseminate one of our heifers. That was over thirty years ago when we lived in Oulu. Then, after college we met again. We were single, it worked," she said. She studied her feet.

"How come you two never got married?"

"Well, we talked about it. But never got around to

it. Then the lake thing came up."

"Lake thing?"

"Well, actually it was the barrels. After a while we got into a lot of fights over the barrel stuff, over the lake. He got to calling her 'My Precious'." Cheney paused.

"I see," Davecki said though he couldn't really see any relevance.

The waves lapped. In the distance, Puddles barked again. He looked up the beach, saw the dog running after a gull that was flying low, teasing the ground-bound pooch. Hazel Cheney shifted herself on the log and emoted heavily. In all his years as a detective, Davecki had learned to sense when someone was considering a confession. He'd learned to repress his impatience at times like these. "Ummmm," he said.

Cheney rubbed her ear. The dangling topaz earring jiggled from the movement. "We broke up a year ago. I wanted to get married and have a baby before it was too late."

"He said no?"

"Well, I was the one who said no actually."

"Why?" Davecki asked.

Cheney rubbed her knee and squeezed her legs together. "Well, he was willing to be the father but not get married."

"Ummm, I see," Davecki said.

Cheney looked at him. "You do?"

"Yeah," he said.

More waves lapping. No Puddles barking in the distance but a long silence. Then Cheney said, "I thought of settling, of just accepting it. But I knew I'd be really pissed if it was just a sperm donor thing."

Davecki looked at her. For the first time he didn't see a suspect. She's innocent, he thought. "So, I gotta ask ya...." Davecki fussed with his jacket. "Why are you here? I mean, why today? It looks bad."

Cheney looked at him. "Yeah. The jilted lover thing. I know. But, to be honest, I was here hoping see him. We used to come out here all the time...you know walk, talk, watch the sunset...."

"Yeah...I know," Davecki interrupted. He didn't want to know more.

"I didn't kill him. No way. When I didn't see his Jeep, I just decided to walk..."

"From where?"

"Down at the lighthouse."

"You walked all that way?"

"It's not that far," Cheney said looking toward town.

Davecki begged to differ but didn't. Instead he tried to get a mental image of Gronsby washing up on shore. The body was up out of the water and there were no waves big enough to toss his two hundred pounds that far up into the sand. The only scene he could conjure was the improbable sight of the Lake Herself spitting Gronsby out like a watermelon seed. No way would he share that vision with anyone. He needed to change the karma of that image so he said, "So you were ready to lower your standards?"

Hazel Cheney placed both her hands on her knees. She spread her legs slightly. "I was considering it. I'm not getting any younger." She paused, drummed her fingers, then continued, "I was also thinking he might have changed, been ready to settle down."

"He's settled down now," Davecki said and he regretted it instantly. Hazel Cheney stopped all her movements. She remained motionless for two seconds and then cupped her face in her own small hands and began a good cry.

6

Davecki knew about good cries. He'd grown up the youngest boy in a family of three women. He put his arm around the shaking shoulders of the Simpering Suzy beside him and indulged himself in a self pitying analysis. He concluded that his entire youth was nothing more than a long sentence of good cries punctuated by the occasional semi-colon of sanity. He recalled the first joke he'd ever made up. It was in High School. He worked on the school paper. His English teacher was out for eight weeks, home recovering from a colostomy. Davecki wrote the headline, "English Teacher Home Recovering with Semi-Colon." It wasn't a big hit with school officials and he was asked to seek other outlets for his creativity.

He felt Hazel move into his chest, felt her sobbing radiate through his ribs and knew there was no defense against the sadness resonating in his own heart. But he knew he could feel it much later and in a much more private setting. For now, he knew, he had a chance to collect his thoughts. He knew he'd get around to grief. It was as inevitable as ice in January. As he grew older, defending himself against his own emotions was tougher. But, he told himself as he clenched his jaw in resolve, he could delay, dodge and manage those distracting, nasty things called feelings until a more appropriate time.

Davecki gazed across the pristine waters. He let his vision go to infinity. Out on the waves three miles away or so he saw a white speck. Charter boat, he thought. He pushed his vision past the visual obstruction and imagined his eyesight as a discernible wave of cosmic energy rushing off across the water just going, going, going, like a quantum physicist's wet dream. His proclivity to ruin a good thing clicked on in his brain and his mind wanted to bring the wave back. Its first trick was to bring up the Energizer Bunny. The wave of vision paused and looked back like Puddles had done. As the vision wave waited, Davecki rehearsed the saying, "The mind is a valuable servant and a terrible master." He envisioned himself pulling his Glock. He drew down on and plugged the pink pounder three times. Soft tufts of fake fur and stuffing exploded like feathers from a pillow fight. His vision wave turned and resumed its surge toward the infinite.

The serenity quest resumed, Davecki was able to relax. He felt Hazel's sobs but they were distant now. They were still physically connected but they were distant. His visioning had distanced the sobs emotionally and he was grateful for having learned the detachment trick from his youthful experiences with hysteric womenfolk. He took note of his breathing. He let his vision range off across the water, but he asked the air to come in. He inhaled and imagined a string of breath three hundred miles long being pulled across all of the lake. He wasn't surprised that the enormous length of breath easily reeled into his own chest.

He noticed the duality of his psychic spectacle. His vision was above, going out and away. His breath was below, coming in. It was like the Oliver Bridge across the St. Louis River. Trains above. Cars below. Both moving in opposite directions, but united in structure. He knew the vision and the breath were moving without conflict or competition and he saw in a second that all the air in the world could get in his chest as long as the vision was going out. Then he knew the vision would eventually return. A milli-second of panic tried to become a full second. Davecki knew that there were hours, days and weeks of fearful panic in his past and that, just for today, no, just for this moment, he didn't have to be afraid of exploding as long as he paid a bit of attention to the balance of vision going out and breath coming in.

Panic vanished.

Davecki began to exhale.

His vision wave turned back languidly. At that moment Davecki felt Hazel's sadness touch his heart and he lowered his chin. He closed his eyes and began an inner recital. *Our Father who art in heaven*, he began. Then he saw Thurber's face rise out of the waters of the far end of Lake Superior. The image of Gronsby was smiling. It joined the vision wave and together they began returning.

Hallowed be Thy name, Davecki said to himself. As he inhaled, the vision and the image drew closer and Davecki knew Thurber was present. Davecki said the entire prayer while letting the face of Gronsby get closer and closer.

"I hope you're happy Thurber," Davecki murmured. He raised his head to see if Hazel had heard him mumble. He was happy to discover that her good cry was still fully engaged. He looked left. Puddles was just a dot way up the beach. He looked right. Strum was videotaping the scene. Bales was waiting with the bag. Hasaan was staring up at the sky. Davecki wondered, was he looking for Jesus' return? Could he see Gronsby too? Davecki looked back at the lake. The white speck of a hull had grown larger. It was a Bertram. He felt stronger. He felt as if his chest was indestructible, as if his lungs were the strongest ceramic tile in the world.

Inside himself he laughed. Why not steel? he questioned inwardly. Being an iconoclast was his trademark. It made him a good detective, which is what he had to be soon. Hazel would cry herself out and he'd have to quiz her up. What did he know so far? Thurber was dead. His body had washed up —or was deposited— he added, on the beach since Hazel had passed. How long ago? An hour? That was fast he thought. If Gronsby floated in, maybe that charter captain had seen something. He twitched involuntarily at his instant urge to call dispatch and get a positive I.D. on the boat. Hazel sensed his twitch and disengaged from his side. He felt her detaching. He wondered, did a big trout feel the same when a lamprey let go?

No wonder I'm single, Davecki thought.

Hazel recomposed herself. She patted her hair and daubed at her cheeks with the backs of both hands. "I'm a mess," she said.

Davecki reached into his inside jacket pocket. He retrieved his tumor-maker and punched the hot key which held Dispatch's number. Bonnie would get the Coast Guard to contact the Bertram. Maybe it was Captain John. John would yank his lines and come over to talk if he knew it was Davecki asking. The phone tone pulsed in his right ear. With his left, he heard Hazel's alarmed, "Puddles?"

"Here, Puddles," Hazel called on his left.

"Hey Davecki," Bonnie said on his right.

Davecki could feel his indestructible chest start to crumble. "Hang on Bonnie," he said.

"Hazel, could you give me a second?" he asked after he'd covered the phone with his left hand.

"Sure," she said. Standing up she looked down the beach. Then she looked toward Superior and said, "I'll find Puddles."

"Don't go far," Davecki commanded.

Hazel walked away and Davecki, before bringing the phone up to his ear, wondered, what kind of person would name a dog Puddles?

"Bon," Davecki said, "could you get the Coasties to contact a charter captain for me?" The cop listened and glanced at Hazel's nice ass swiveling down the beach. "Sure," he said. "It's a white Bertram. Could be the Formula. There aren't many Bertrams around."

Davecki listened. He kicked at the sand, made two deep troughs with his heels. "Okay hon, thanks. Call back quick." Davecki answered.

He punched end and stood. In the distance Puddles was running toward Hazel's calls of, "Here girl."

"Hey Dave," Bale's voice came at him from behind. In front of him he saw the big dumb dog jump up on its owner's chest with its front paws. "Lucky dog, lucky dog," Davecki said mimicking the old commercial. When he saw the pair turn back toward him, he turned toward the crime scene. Bales was approaching. He had left the body bag and was holding something shiny.

"You screwing with evidence Bales?"

The uniform looked meanly at him. "Not that you care," Bales said gesturing with his chin past Davecki's shoulder.

"Up your's Bales. What'cha got?"

O'Baily laughed. "It's a seaman's card."

Davecki recalled the Moby Blow Job joke about the whale biting the end off the submarine and sucking out all the seamen. "Lemme see," he said reaching out. Bales handed him a laminated I.D. card that was weathered and battered looking. "It was in the sand," he said.

"Buried?" Davecki asked looking at the card.

"I guess. I don't know."

"What do you mean, you don't know?"

"Lighten up," Bales shot back.

Davecki tried to ease up, but his chest was getting hard in a brittle way. "Don't tell me how to be," he said, "If it was buried, maybe he buried it. Maybe he was alive when he got here."

"No shit Shakespeare," Bales said. "How am I supposed to know if the damn thing was buried? All I know is the card sort of appeared in the sand when we started stuffing him."

Something in the Water

"Sorry, Bales," Davecki said as Hazel and the Jumper walked up. Dave knew he would call the dog Jumper after seeing those big paws on her front. What sort of person would name a dog Jumper? he wondered, what sort of person could have so many thoughts in his head at one time?

Hazel stopped and stood between the two cops. Her face was tear streaked, but Davecki noted, her eyes were less sad.

"Bales found a card," Davecki said handing the merchant marine document to the woman. Puddles stuck her nose in Davecki's crotch so fast he couldn't defend his jewels. "Fucking dog!" Davecki yelped and smacked the creature hard on the nose with his fist. The dog yelped loudly and jumped backwards.

Bales laughed.

"You hurt her!" Hazel said.

"I hate when a bitch does that without asking first!" Bales joked.

Davecki was shaking the pain from his hand when his pocket started chirping. He pulled out his phone, punched any key and said, "Yeah." He listened and looked out to the Big Lake. Sure enough the boat was coming closer. "Thanks Bonnie," he said and punched the phone out before stuffing it away.

"Poor baby," Cheney was saying to Puddles. The dog glared at Davecki with a "What the hell did I do wrong?" look and sneezed.

Bales, seeing that Cheney wasn't looking, grabbed his crotch and hauled his equipment around, a big grin on his face. "Sore on the shore," he said.

40

"Huh?" Hazel said looking up just as Bales quickly removed his hand.

"He's coming ashore," Davecki nodded toward the lake.

Both O'Baily and Cheney looked out to see. "Who?" Bales asked.

"Captain John Chuckson, the best charter captain on the lake. Maybe he saw something." Davecki stated.

"From that distance?" Bales asked.

"Ever hear of binoculars?"

"Now, boys," Hazel said.

The men stared at each other for three seconds until Cheney said slowly, "I think I know the guy on this card."

Davecki turned to see her proffering the I.D. He reached out quickly and snatched it. The card snapped loudly as it exchanged hands.

"Who?" is all Davecki asked.

The rumble of the charter boat's engines intruded across the water as Cheney said, "Well, I'm not sure. But it looks a lot like a young Brooks Robertson to me."

"Who the hell is Brooks Robertson," Davecki questioned. His breathing was getting shallower. He wanted to hold his nuts. Puddles, he realized had banged her sniffing nose into his right testicle, the one he was convinced was cancerous. He was pissed at Bales for his gesture and now he had another suspect.

"Brooks Robertson is an old guy at the home

where I work." Hazel answered softly. "The photo on the card looks like him."

Davecki was staring at the I.D. He moved it closer to his face and then farther away.

"Why don't you just get glasses?" Bales smirked.

He wanted to say, up your's Bales, but he didn't want to give the mere squadman any more satisfaction. Instead he said, "Well, if this is a photo of Brooks Robertson, then why does the card have the name Lars Knudson printed on it?

"You're the detective," Bales said as he turned away.

Behind him a voice came across the water. "Hello the beach!"

Davecki turned to see a gorgeous twenty-six foot Bertram gliding across the water toward the beach. The captain stood on the flying bridge and shouted again, "Hello the beach! What can I do for you, Dave?" his old friend shouted. The low rumble of one of the boat's twin six-cylinder engines died.

The faces of the bewildered looking party of two sport fishermen and two sport fisherwomen standing on the lower deck modulated from confusion to shock when Davecki shouted, "You can help me solve a murder, Chucky-baby!"

"Hot damn!" Chuckson yelled and he practically killed himself throwing his six foot four inch frame down the chrome ladder to the gunwales.

Davecki regretted his predisposition to blurting out information that was best left unsaid.

7

Captain John had been fishing on Lake Superior, as he put it, "Since before dirt." The big Swede was a prototype Nordic warrior. At six foot four and weighing two forty, he possessed all the physical prowess of a bear. He also had the bear's demeanor. Slow to anger, but you most certainly did not want to piss him off. He was blonde, handsome and mostly quiet. He was observant in the discreet way of all Scandinavians. His father, John Chuckson, III, had him sport fishing on the Big Lake when he was, "Just a tadpole." Chuckson and Davecki met at an ice fishing contest while competing for a woman. Davecki won the fishing match by catching a four pound lawyer, the ugliest, most slime laden fish in the lake. Chuckson won the woman and made friends with Davecki. It was an unlikely friendship in several ways. Davecki was an old commercial fisherman from down the lake. Chuckson was a sporter who —Davecki's hometown clan in Cornucopia felt— was at least partially if not fully responsible for the DNR's decision to eradicate commercial fishing on Lake Superior. Davecki's neighbor in his home town, Alphonse Celinski, had said, "Dem richy riches wit dair big boats 'n wallets got all doze poly-tickle connectshuns." Which was to say politicians, bureaucrats and special interest groups conspired to ruthlessly eradicate an entire culture with the same callousness and ignorance as the ethnic cleansing in Bosnia. Davecki's real name wasn't Alphonse for nothing.

Something in the Water

The sweeping prow of the Formula swung around to the southeast as if Captain John was steering the boat using telekinetic powers. Chuckson was one of a handful of charter captains who could pilot a boat safely across the many shallow sand bars present on the "Wisconsin side." He also had the reputation as the "fish gettingest charter captain on the western end." This put a lot of high paying customers across his transom. "Fishin's much hotter when Chuckson's on the water," his brochure read.

Which was mostly all the time, being on the water that is. Davecki knew Chuckson was always out early, always yanking lines later than all the rest, which explained why they were out so late this evening. The boat was always full of paying customers because of its reputation as a fish-getter. So many people on board meant high bag limits which meant the Formula was able to stay out longer. And, even if the day's charter was limited-out, Chuckson's tender way with hooked lake trout and salmon made sure the live well held very few dead fish. The charming Captain could most always convince passengers to keep going for trophy fish.

"Got your call from the Coast Guard," Chuckson called across the ten yards of water between the boat and shore. "What can I do you for?"

Davecki eyed the tourists beside Captain John and remembered the sensitivity classes the tourism board presented to the force. Attendance was mandatory because the Mayor was determined to milk the tourists for all the money she could. Appropriate for the

Dairy State, Davecki thought. He knew Chuckson would beach the boat and disembark if he asked him to, but he didn't want to ask such a favor. Little choppy waves were building and he felt the wind picking up out of the north. It could roughen up the passengers if a goodly chop blew in, plus Davecki didn't want to jeopardize the Captain's income any more than he already had. The boat was drifting along straight and parallel to the shore and Davecki suddenly realized John hadn't made a move for the ship's wheel. The cop bent over and squinted, peering through the windows of the cutty cabin. What he saw explained the boat's obedience. Chuckson's wife, Willow, was at the helm. The beautiful woman took her stare off her piloting duties long enough to see Davecki had seen her. She waved, smiled and quickly looked back to her steering. Davecki knew the boat was in good hands and felt free to ask the Captain ashore.

"Can you come ashore, John?"

"Sure thing," Chuckson answered without hesitation. "Will honey, nose her in and I'll bail off the bow."

The boat clunked its innards in response to the Captain's commands and started pivoting its bow toward the shore. Chuckson was hauling his frame along the gunwale toward the bow. By the time he reached the nose, the prow was kissing sand. Chuckson leapt off the boat, landed heavily with both feet and the boat backed away as if the maneuver had been rehearsed hundreds of times.

"Hey Dave, What'sup?" Chuckson said approaching the group, extending his hand.

The two men shook hands.

"Gronsby's gone," Davecki answered.

"Croaked?"

"Yeah," Davecki said,

Hazi made a whimpering sound.

"John, this is Hazel Cheney. You know Officer O'Baily, I think," Davecki said,

"Hey Bales," Chuckson said half waving at the blue. He extended the same hand toward Hazi. "Nice to meet'cha," he said in greeting.

Hazi stuck out her hand and they shook.

"Seen any action over this way in the last hour or so, Chuck?"

"Not a bite. Not a whisper of a bite," the Captain answered instantly.

"Any radio chatter?" Davecki asked.

"Nada."

"You been fishing or on the flying bridge?"

"Fishing mostly. Willow's been driving."

Davecki looked at the boat standing patiently off shore. "So you could have missed a boat coming in?" Davecki asked.

"Naw, I don't think so, Dave."

"Why's that?"

Chuckson shifted his large moccasin-clad feet in the sand, "There's only five guys out today and four of them are working the Minnesota side. My people didn't want to buy Minnesota day tickets. They're all from Appleton and had Wisconsin licenses already. I've been dancing along the state line and would have noticed someone coming in."

Davecki knew John Chuckson. He'd fished often with the Captain. No charge of course. There had to be <u>some</u> bennys to policework. If Chuckson said there had been no boat ashore here in the last hour, then that was fact as far as Davecki was concerned and that meant Gronsby's body had come to Wisconsin Point either floating or by land.

"Hey Chuck, thanks for coming over. Sorry about the interruption. Sorry about the murder comment. Shouldn't have blurted that out."

"The Mayor's gonna send your ass to another class," Chuckson said flashing a grin.

"How's she going to find out?"

"Beat's me. But with your rep as a joker you could probably beat the rap by saying you were just goofing around."

"I was," Davecki said raising his hands, "Body? What body?"

"You're such a tease," Chuckson said turning toward the water. "Bring 'er in honey," he yelled and waved the boat toward the shore.

The boat thunked loudly as the Merc-Cruiser was put in gear. The hull glided through the building chop as Davecki asked, "You ever hear of a guy named Brooks Robertson, John?"

Chuckson turned and said, "Big time union operative for years. Haven't heard much about him for a long time though. I think he retired."

The boat's nose nudged the sand and Chuckson grabbed the bow rail and jumped, pulling himself deftly aboard. Chuckson stood on the foredeck as the boat backed away.

Something in the Water

"I won't say a word to the Mayor at the dinner party tonight," he said and grinned again. "If you need any more help, let me know. At least now," he said nodding down the beach toward Strum and the body bag, "we won't have to be worrying about those barrels coming up."

Davecki watched as the Formula departed. He knew Chuckson and all the charter captains hated Gronsby. Actually, Davecki corrected his thinking, they hated Gronsby's plan, his crusade to raise every last one of the mysterious barrels and "rid the Crown Jewel of the Great Lakes of those blasphemous barrels," as Thurber so eloquently soundbited every time a TV camera was on. Davecki knew the captains didn't want to risk disturbing the barrels and thereby contaminating their fishing grounds. Davecki wondered why Gronsby decided to raise such a flap about the barrels. He'd started his busy body career by concentrating on managing the city forest by press release. But then his focus switched to the barrels and he became relentless. Having heard Hazel Cheney's story, Davecki knew Gronsby was obsessed.

Davecki waved as the powerful engines surged and the boat began to plane out. He saw Captain John talking to his charters. The boatman was standing in the middle of the aft deck gesturing freely with both hands. His audience, each and every one, was clutching to every handrail available. Chuckson had the best sea legs in the business. Plus he had the best pilot driving the boat today.

Davecki lowered his arm and turned toward the

last remains of Thurber Gronsby. He led Hazi and Bales toward the body and thought about Chuckson and his buddies. They didn't want something from the barrels getting into the water. Davecki eyed the black bag. Gronsby didn't want the barrels in the water at all. The barrels were in the water. There was something in the barrels. Gronsby had been in the water. Somebody wanted Gronsby, wrapped in an old gill net, in the water.

There it was, he concluded, as it always was and ever more shall be around Lake Superior.... The water, the water, the water, always with the water. Was something in the water that could point Davecki to Gronsby's killer? He couldn't even begin to imagine what as the phone in his pocket chirped.

8

It takes at least a week for a forensics report to get done in Superior, Wisconsin. One reason for the delay is that the autopsy is performed in St. Paul. A rookie has to transport the body and be present for the slicing and dicing. The report is faxed to the appropriate offices and the stiff is returned to the rightful owners. Davecki was a rookie once and the experience soured him on dead bodies forever, a fact for which he was deeply grateful. He certainly didn't want to be the owner of one of those subtle attractions to dead people that a couple of his co-workers had. He was lucky. His first corpse wasn't some luscious whore found dead in a massage parlor tied up in a lurid position. He'd heard plenty of cop-talk about the nasty nature of **those** dreams.

Davecki's first dead body had sat on the toilet for a week in August before the neighbor lady in the downstairs apartment at 2102 Ogden called in a complaint about the smell. If she'd called any other city office she wouldn't have been a suspect in the young cop's mind. Standing around in the second floor apartment waiting for the detective in charge to make up his mind about moving the body, Davecki didn't think the copshop was the first place a guiltless person would call about a stench. Then he noticed the old guy's tea had left a crystalline residue behind when it evaporated. She got life in prison for serving the old guy strychnine with his Oolong. Fortunately for her she was an old witch too. She died three weeks into her sentence at the Wisconsin State Prison for Women in Taycheedah. For his excellence, Davecki got a reputation for noticing the little things and was rewarded with the opportunity to help bag a corpse that fell apart to the touch. Lovely.

His hyper vigilance became a constant when he was promoted to detective and it grew in intensity with each investigation. However, an ancillary effect grew alongside his obsession for detail. He could be certifiably out to lunch when over-focused on a case. This oblivion was in full bloom as Davecki sat at the stop light on Catlin and Belknap. He'd just come from the Donut Shop. He was thinking about what the waitress Rita had told him. He was thinking about his need to go to visit the Reservation in Red Cliff. He was planning to talk to Randy Salmon Slayer. Slayer was the Great Lakes Indian Fish and Wildlife Crick Dick who knew every legal and illegal gill netter from Ontonagan, Michigan to the Canadian end of Lake of the Woods. All this was on his mind when it gradually became apparent to him that a horn was tooting behind him. He was instantly ready to give the inconsiderate SOB the finger when he realized the light was green and he'd been lost in thought. He was glad he'd restrained himself. He hated wasting perfectly decent obscene gestures on innocent parties. Davecki looked in the rear-view mirror and saw a beautiful woman in a blue Ford Escort. She looked familiar. She waved. He put the Stang in gear and headed south.

He was on his way to Lost Creek Health facility to talk to Brooks Robertson. Rita at the donut shop had heard of the union man. Said he was a tug boat man and on-call thug for a stevedore named Kerry Koskinen. Davecki was glad to have learned while investigating the murder of a longshoreman, that stevedore's were not longshoremen. The stevedore was just a middle link in the chain of command that got things done on the waterfront. In fact it was the unusually well informed Rita who had to explain the difference to him. Rita knew a lot about everything and she was always ready to loudly share her opinions. She'd worked at the Donut House forever. She was short, small, sassy and smart. In other words she was a great source. Davecki liked talking with her ever since they'd argued about a bill and she brazenly advised him to, "Go to hell," in front of twenty-five patrons. He put a high reliability factor on any information she handed out. She said Koskinen's boss was Nick Navarone and stated boldly that, if there was wickedness at work, it was trickle down evil for sure.

He shifted into third and nosed the Mustang into the newly designed Catlin Avenue which wound through the University. Why they screwed up a perfectly good street that was straight and wide by putting in a bunch of silly curves, Davecki couldn't understand. He looked at the uninspiring buildings of his alma mater and suspected the money could have been more well spent on student services or even to hire yet another pompous academic for the History Department. He suspected there was probably some little king or queen ruling a bureaucratic fifedom that could sway a huge amount of money into what amounted to bloated landscaping. But, while it was his business to be suspicious, while he was actually paid to be paranoid, it most certainly wasn't his business to judge the goings on at the state's most anemic academic outpost.

His business was to catch Thurber's killer. It was official now. The autopsy confirmed the cause of death as drowning and that Gronsby's estimated T.O.D. had made him dead for three days before he was found. It was clear that The Gron had floated into his beloved Wisconsin Point.

Just as Gronsby loved the Point, one of Davecki's favorite places was his Mustang. Like Mae West, he was best while moving. He thought best while driving. "Okay," he said out loud. He pounded the steering wheel twice as he drove past the Fine Arts building. He looked at the rider's seat and grabbed a piece of crumpled paper lying there. On it six lines were written. They were: 1. Thurber is dead. 2. He drowned. 3. He had a false I.D. with Robertson's picture on it. 4. Suspect number one, Hazel Cheney. 5. Suspect number two, half the Chippewa Nation. Under line five was an a. followed by the words, Outdated gill net as murder weapon. 6. Suspect number three Something in the Water. The fourth line was crossed out.

Davecki downshifted for the stop sign at Twenty-first street. He was planning a rolling stop when a spunky looking Wrangler refused to let him go first. The green Jeep was driven by a brunette with hair like Liza Minelli in Cabaret. Davecki sighed and stepped on the brake. The Jeep driver laughed obviously and sped across in front of him waving as she went. She held a tube of lipstick between her fingers.

He waved and drove on. At the University building of Hawkes Hall he heard the beep behind him again. It was a pathetic excuse for a horn with a grating little beep instead of a hearty honk. The miserable noise irritated him. He looked in the mirror and saw the Escort babe was still there. She turned right into the parking lot and he said aloud, "Oh yeah. The CASDA lady." The woman worked at the Center Against Sexual and Domestic Abuse. She was always at headquarters filing papers to bust abuser ass.

Davecki drove south and then east and south again until he was on the open road heading toward Lost Creek Home fifteen miles distant. He thought about Hazel Cheney as he tugged the steering wheel. He was doing seventy-five around one of his favorite on-camber corners just past the E-Z bar near the Wisconsin Central pulp loading yard. While awaiting the autopsy, Davecki had interviewed her. She didn't have any alibi at all for the time period in which Gronsby was killed. "That's *another* bad thing about living alone," she'd said. Despite her inability to account for her whereabouts, he concluded with certainty that Hazel wasn't guilty. Weak motive. A woman jilted can be murderous he thought, as he slowed to forty-five miles-an-hour for Nakoma Gardens, but her values regarding a baby precluded her from the murder. Plus, a woman with her good looks could always find a husband. It was the less comely ones who often became so panicked that they killed. Davecki looked left at his favorite brown house in the tall pines.

As the beautiful house swooshed by he moved down his list of suspects. It was unlikely that an Indian had killed Gronsby, Dave thought as he passed highway K and pushed down on the gas pedal. Though it was too early in the investigation to exclude a race thing, there were no solid leads pointing to a tribal motive. Besides, the Shinobs were mostly in favor of cleaning up the lake. And there were no accident reports of Gronsby rear-ending any Indian cars in Duluth, so that angle was weak. But that gill net. Davecki knew, having grown up in a fishing village, that only Indian fishermen were allowed such free rein that any net would do. "Oh well," Davecki said aloud. He wondered if such ejaculations constituted talking to himself.

He'd taken to calling his verbal spouts ejaculations after the short prayers he was forced to utter in Catholic school. He looked at the St. Christopher medal and wondered where prayer cards had gone.

At the sight of the big white pine by Dreamland Supper Club, Davecki made an unusual decision. He turned right and go over the top of Sam Anderson hill. He braked hard and reined the Mustang through the off-camber turn and across the railroad tracks.

He hadn't, he knew as he shifted back up through the gears, listed Robertson as a suspect because of an ironclad alibi. He was incarcerated. He had been locked up at Lost Creek Home for the last three years according to Hazel Cheney. "He did wander. But we put the bracelet on and he stopped," she offered. He couldn't have killed Gronsby. But, Davecki hoped as he drove past the wooden wolf sculptures on the left, perhaps old Brooks could shed some light on the "sitshee-ation," as Davecki's Dad often called a dilemma. Even if he didn't know anything about the murder, Robertson sure had some explaining to do regarding the false I.D.

Hazel had agreed to meet with Davecki and Robertson to help Dave sort out the old man's responses. His dementia, Hazel explained, was getting worse, but as she'd worked at Lost Creek since before Robertson was dumped there by his ingrate kids, she'd heard most of his disjointed stories while they still made some sense.

"Maybe I can help," she volunteered.

"Maybe," Davecki said as he replayed the scene of her tank top not topping when he'd first seen her on the beach. He wondered if her willingness to help had something to do with her desire to have a baby. He made plans not to smile at her even once.

Davecki weaved the Mustang across the bridge over the Amnicon River and drove out onto Old 53, disobeying the stop sign just beyond the Wisconsin Central tracks. There were no green Jeeps around this time. He stomped on the gas while the rear wheels were still on the pea gravel and they squealed in delight. The rest of the way to the home he pondered what sort of man perceived tires as squealing with delight and how that differed from naming a dog Puddles. He knew any distraction was a good thing because he could be as obsessive as Gronsby.

9

"**D**amn," Davecki said as he turned right into the long driveway of Lost Creek Home. Usually the only sight to greet a visitor to the old TB Sanitarium turned nursing home was the massive stone structure in the distance. The building had an imposing quality that reminded Davecki of the hotel in *The Shining*. Today however, upon turning the corner, Davecki saw something that made his stomach clench and it wasn't Jack Nicholson. It was George Plimpton. The hood was looking under the upraised hood of his black '77 Pontiac 6000. Steam rose. Plimpton was looking at the steam. His hands were on his narrow hips.

Davecki slowed the Mustang and jabbed the power window button.

"Hey George," Davecki said loudly over the exhaust rumble of the Stang's forty-thousandths over-bored port fuel injected 302.

Plimpton turned around smiling. When he saw who greeted him, his face fell into pitiful. Davecki had seen it a million times. The woe, the tragedy, the bad luck. It was the, "officer you wouldn't believe how horrible life has been to me," look. Copshop talk called it, *doing pitiful*.

"Dave!" Plimpton said mixing genuine surprise into a bitter-batter recipe of fear and loathing.

"George," Davecki said. "Need any help?"

"Naw, I'm just waiting for her to cool down so I can whack the thermostat. It's stuck."

Davecki looked around. The pine plantation across

the field radiated a lively green aura. The sky above the lush hardwoods on the right was pale blue. He sighed. "How did that vehicle get here, George?"

The punk fidgeted. "Theresa drove from home. She walked back to the nursing home for water."

"She have the baby yet?"

"Naw. She's big as a house. Won't let me touch her."

She shouldn't have in the first place, Davecki thought. "You still revoked?"

Plimpton flinched at the question. "Yeah."

"Don't let me see you driving George," Davecki said. He dumped the clutch and burped a blatt from the new fifteen inch Cooper tires on the Stang's rear axle. He hated people who pushed the system, pushed the envelope of tolerance. Plimpton had Davecki's sympathies. No, Theresa had Davecki's sympathies. Knocked up at seventeen. Husband who lived with his new wife in a run-down trailer in a field next to a logged-off forty. Davecki had let Plimpton get away with driving while revoked so many times it was laughable. Only, as Davecki pulled up to the nursing home, he wasn't laughing.

An incongrous little girl was, like Elvis, leaving the building. It was Theresa McGrath. Her gut stuck out like a huge balloon under an oversized man's shirt that hung loosely around the skinny shoulders of the stick-figure. Davecki pounded his steering wheel twice. "Bam! Bam!" There was no rhythm and the dash shook.

Theresa was carrying two ice cream pails. Water

sloshed out of both of them as she walked. The detective left the motor running as she walked out from under the Home's canopy. He popped the trunk with the glove compartment button, got out and said to the waif with the water, "Let me help."

Theresa smiled. She looked at him with *a look*. It was as if she *knew* he would show up.

Davecki felt stirring in his guts. The feeling never failed. Every time he saw a pregnant woman he felt a deep clenching in his stomach. Should he have had kids? He'd decided early in his life that the answer was no. He was seventeen. The same age as Theresa. He admired Gronsby for never marrying. Cop life is tough on families. He dumped water from each bucket onto the blacktop to minimize spilling. He put the buckets in, closed the lid. He'd have to drive extra slow to keep the water inside the buckets.

"How'zit going?" he asked as he opened the door for the whale-fronted scarecrow. She looked at him without saying anything. She had big brown eyes. He didn't want to look into them. But it would be impolite not to look at all. He cursed his mother for pounding the ordinance of politeness toward women into him during his tenure as a part time boy/part time object of rage. He knew he couldn't look too long or he would want to save this one.

"Fine," Theresa said.

Davecki's glance into her eyes caused his guts to clench again. He closed the door on her, got in and drove slowly back to the Pontiac. "What brings you to Lost Creek?" he asked.

Something in the Water

"Visiting Grampa Brooks," Theresa said.

Davecki felt blessed. "Your Grandfather is Brooks Robertson?"

The pregnant little woman folded her petite hands into a praying gesture in the small lap in front of her enormous belly. "Yep. He's the greatest. Or, was the greatest. Before that barrel crap got into him!"

"Barrel crap?" Davecki asked. Suddenly he wanted something completely out of character. He wished the Mustang could go slower.

"Yeah. You know. Those Gronsby barrels. Daddy said that Grampa Brooks got contaminated by that pink barrel goop that spilled and it made him go demented."

Davecki wanted to ask her why her last name was McGrath. Didn't. Instead he said, "Does your Dad know Thurber Gronsby?" Davecki thought he might have another suspect.

Theresa flicked her interwoven fingers. "Yep. But he's been in Dillingham fishing since the first of June."

"Ummmm," Davecki said. She seemed to suspect his suspicions. Only seventeen and so worldly wise he thought. She glanced at him. The look seemed to say that Davecki knew only the half of it. "How's the season up there?" he asked.

She laughed a little snorting laugh. "Pretty good, Mom says. When he called on the satellite phone last week he said they chased a Jap boat out of Bristol Bay."

Davecki idled up to the Pontiac, stopped the Mustang as gently as he could and started to reach over to open the glove box and pop the trunk. He smelled her and stopped. "Just open the glove box and push the yellow button Theresa," he said.

Davecki ejected himself and went around to the trunk.

"What took ya Terry?" George said from under the hood of his junker. Theresa was struggling out of the Mustang's cramped front seat. Davecki lifted the buckets. Water was sloshed all over his carpeting. He hated messing up his car, but he had to help Theresa. "George!" Davecki called. "Come here."

"Yeah, yeah." Plimpton said.

Theresa went to the passenger's side of the Pontiac and got in the car. Davecki knew from a previous stop that she'd never gotten her driver's license. He stood between the white ice-cream pails at his feet and glared at Plimpton as the boy approached. "That's all you got?" he asked.

Davecki wanted to grab him, throw him down and kick his ass. "Straighten up and fly right," was what he said.

Plimpton looked at him confused. Davecki realized the kid didn't have a clue. He also realized the saying that just popped out of his mouth was his father's and so distant from Plimpton's reality that its effect was nothing more than wasted breath. "Get it together," Davecki said and slammed the trunk. Plimpton looked blank. Davecki got in the car without a word and forced himself not to burn thirty thousand miles of tread off the new tires as he returned to the business of visiting Brooks Robertson and finding out who murdered Thurber Gronsby. As he returned to the looming edifice of Lost Creek Home, Davecki focused on breathing deeply and wondered if he'd failed or passed the test of character just now. It was hard to know sometimes. It was the nineties, not the sixties. Back then giving Plimpton a good thrashing would have been appropriate. These days such an attitude adjustment would just get him debadged and get Plimpton a barge-load of cash when the Department settled out of court. Davecki sighed again and tapped twice on the steering wheel. The dash didn't rattle. It felt good to have the final two raps on the steering wheel in. He hardly knew it himself, but four beats on the steering wheel was a mantra for him. Two beats on the wheel meant things were going poorly. Four meant resolution. He summoned a vision of Lake Superior's glistening waters. The waves were small. The sun was shining. There was only the slightest wind.

His breathing deepened and he shut the Mustang off. He looked down the long sidewalk leading to Lost Creek. He knew George and Theresa had a Higher Power of their own. He had to let go of their problems and concentrate on Robertson. He was eager to talk to the old salt. It had been a long time since he'd had any contact with a man of the sea. He was eager to revisit his days as a commercial fisherman. He was looking forward to some seafaring chatter.

10

Davecki walked into the lobby of the nursing home. On the left, beyond closed double doors, a congregation of white heads, some in wheel chairs, others in rows of steel folding chairs, were singing, "On a hill far away stood an old rugged cross." Davecki walked past the doors and approached a blue Formica counter on the right. In the office beyond the counter a woman sat behind a desk cluttered with papers. She didn't look up. She was humming the melody of the hymn.

"Is Hazel Cheney in? She's expecting me," Davecki said.

The woman twitched in surprise and blurted out, "Oh! No. No, she's not here now. She had to rush home because her husband was attacked by a rototiller."

"What?"

The woman smiled. Her teeth were straight and white. "He was tilling or something and got his leg caught I guess," she said. "Hazi had to go bandage him up. She'll be back later I think."

"Well, I was supposed to see Brooks Robertson," Davecki said.

The lady behind the counter was cute. Of course, to Davecki, all women were cute or beautiful or luscious or pretty or some such thing. He remembered F.C. Abernathy the five hundred pound former shipping clerk who killed a Sri Lankan sailor by sitting on him for twenty minutes. The skinny guy stopped breathing. When the cops arrived at the office on the old Sivertson slip near the Harvest States grain elevator, Davecki asked the unruffled fat woman what happened. She replied calmly that the man initiated "Unwarranted touching." It was a complicated case involving the use of excessive force in response to a dubious threat. Davecki had to conduct a lot of interviews. Once, F.C., speaking in her unflappable manner, made an offhanded comment to the effect that she was, "Safe in here." It took a while, but Davecki figured out she meant inside herself and not inside the jail. When they took her from the courtroom after the conviction, F.C. flashed a smile at Davecki at the last moment and he saw what she was, what she really was, a gorgeous woman afraid of her own beauty who covered it up with hundreds of pounds of concealing flesh.

Shaking off the chilling memory, Davecki wondered why he didn't lust after this clerk. Sometimes yes. Sometimes no. This time no. He leaned over onto the blue Formica counter and remembered his bomber problem. He squeezed his arms together to push the jacket closed at the front and keep his weapon concealed. Once at the Spur station on Hammond Avenue and Broadway, he'd leaned over, shown his hardware inadvertently. The clerk, a nineteen year old blonde, called the cops on him. He got teased a ton for that. The blues on the force wouldn't let it rest for weeks.

"Mr.Robertson's on the third floor. I'll call Melody. She can help you," the bloun haired woman said. Davecki remembered when his sister, Amy, colored her hair once. It didn't turn out so well. Kinda blond. Kinda brown. They'd decided it was bloun.

"No need to bother," Davecki said. "I can find him."

"No bother at all," Bloundie said picking up the phone.

She's too eager, Davecki thought and figured he must have passed the C.G.A. He backed off the counter like a ship standing just off the dock and watched the woman pick up the phone and dial fast. He smiled. It was true.

One good thing about growing up with a shitload of women is, you learned girl stuff. He was ten when he first heard about C.G.A. His sister worked at the school and the secretary/receptionist would always page the single teachers on staff advising them to, "come to the office for your C.G.A. form please." Because he was a geek as a child, it had taken Davecki a couple of decades to trigger a Cute Guy Alert. But now he was just going to enjoy it. After all, he had been wrong in his self-appraisals many times.

"Would you sign in please, sir," the bloun woman said. "Melody will be right down. She's the social worker." The woman pointed at a clipboard on the counter and smiled.

Davecki smiled back and signed in. He moved to a green vinyl-cushioned love seat that could hold two people sitting if they were chummy. A new hymn began in the room behind him. "Rock of Ages cleft for me, let me hide myself in Thee," echoed through the walls and around the foyer. An old man walked by. Actually he shuffled by. White stubble stuck out from his chin. Thin tufts of white hair jutted out from his skull. Wide brown suspenders held green pants high on his waist. "Got to meelk dem cowse," the man said as he passed the reception window.

"You don't have cows anymore Einer," the bloun woman's voice answered. The old guy waved his arm in a sharp gesture of dismissal and kept heading for the door. Davecki heard a chair scrape. The woman's voice called out, "Mr. Koski, you'll trip the alarm!" The blue door alongside the window jerked open and the lady hustled after Mr. Koski. She was shoeless. Koski was shuffling fast now. Davecki wondered if the woman's name might be Jo Jackson.

"Mr. Koski!" the lady called.

The old man reached his left arm out toward the door. An awful electronic alarm started squawking just as the woman caught the perp.

Quite a high speed chase, Davecki thought. The woman grabbed Koski, pulled his arm down and held him tightly against her side. He started chuckling instantly. The woman reached to a keypad on the wall and jabbed four beige keys. Five, two, six, eight, Davecki memorized. The raucous alarm went off. It sounded more like a jail-house riot bell than a nursing home alert. The hymn continued in the next room, "From Thy riven side was shed..." Mr. Koski was still chuckling, Davecki noticed a twinkle in the old guy's eyes that hadn't been there earlier. Bloundie held him close.

He grinned and reached for her chest.

"Dirty old man, you," Bloundie said sharply and slapped Mr. Koski's hand away.

"Heh, heh, heh," Koski said.

Davecki thought of Beavis and Butthead. Then he heard his sister's voice in his head. "A man thinks of sex once every seven seconds."

"Mr. K? Up to your old tricks again?" A new voice entered the fray from stage left. Davecki turned to see a tall black haired woman walking down the hall. She was five-eight if an inch, had a wide face and a radiant smile. She wore dark blue pumps with navy dress and a creamy ivory sweater. She walked up to Koski and cupped his cheek with her hand. "No cows anymore, Mr. K.," she said and she bussed him on the forehead.

Mr. K stopped Beavising and glowed, obedient to the affectionate newcomer. His face shone like the Sand Island light. "I can take care of him, Mel," Bloundie said nodding toward Davecki.

Melody turned toward Davecki and smiled. Sometimes yes, he said to himself. Koski was no fool to submit to this one. Davecki stood, stuck out his hand and said, "I'm Dave Davecki."

"Melody Breedy," the woman said taking Davecki's hand.

He felt her firm grip and let go quickly. Too much voltage. Inwardly he cursed his addiction. Outwardly he said, "I'd like to talk to Brooks Robertson."

"Official police business?" Breedy said lowering her abandoned hand.

"That obvious?"

"No," the woman said. "We've met before."

"Really?" Davecki said.

"I worked my way through UW-Superior doing the C-store thing."

"You?" Davecki asked. "You were blonde then!"

"I know, but it <u>was</u> me," Breedy said. "Never called the cops on a cop before."

"Well, you did right, ma'am," Davecki said stepping back a half step.

"Call me Mel please. I'll take you upstairs but I have to warn you. Mr. Robertson doesn't make a lot of sense most of the time."

"How so?" Davecki asked falling into step alongside the woman. As her heels hit the linoleum floor her bust bounded up and down. He looked away.

"Dementia. Some days are better than others," she said reaching out to push the elevator button.

Inside the box, they rose in silence. Davecki inhaled the urine smell and wondered if Melody was aware of the odor. At the third floor, the bell chimed. The doors clunked open awkwardly. She led him to the right, took another quick right, passed a nursing station and proceeded down a long hall. At room three twenty six, she paused at the half open door. "Brooksie?" she called.

"In a minute," a youthful man's voice responded.

"It'll be just a moment," Melody said to Davecki and stepped away from the door.

She positioned herself under a photo, a quite good photo of an osprey on a nest. Davecki knew the picture was too good to be anything but a Jarvis. He was a local hero among photographers. Slaved away on the railroad all the while making wildlife photos in his spare time and finally got noticed by National Geographic.

"This about Gronsby?" Melody asked.

The woman *was* high voltage. "Yeah," Davecki answered.

"Brooksie's been talking about it, or what passes as talking."

Davecki stepped closer to the woman to let a tall cart of laundry get past. It was being pushed by a trim woman whose name tag said Dorinda. "What's he been saying?"

Breedy reclined into the wall. She rested her back on the pink paint below the osprey and propped her elbows on the yellow hardwood handrail. Davecki saw both the osprey and the woman as equally beautiful. He wondered if he'd have the guts to name a child Osprey. Osprey Davecki.... He was brought back to reality by her answer. "I read the Shipping News to Brooksie every week," Breedy was saying. "Whenever there's any mention of the barrels, he starts in with the Gordon Lightfoot song."

"Huh?" Davecki said.

"He starts singing, 'Lake Superior you know doesn't give up her dead' whenever there's news of the barrels," Breedy explained.

"That's strange," Davecki said.

"Not really," Breedy countered. "Brooksie was a tug boat captain. He ran the Kentucky when it was pulling barges for the barrel dumping."

"How do you know all this?" Davecki asked. He hadn't stepped back after the cart had passed.

Breedy smiled and raised herself from the wall perch. "Thurber Gronsby used to visit Brooksie lots. I'd sit in to interpret just like now," she said smiling broadly. She had straight white teeth and medium thick lips.

"So I should really be interviewing you?" Davecki said.

"Well, I know a lot about Brooksie after five years of being friends," she said.

"What about Hazel Cheney?" Davecki asked.

"What about her?"

"Well," Davecki hesitated. For some reason he didn't want to ask the question in his head.

Breedy smiled. "Could she kill....could she have killed Gronsby?"

Davecki was beginning to sense he was over matched, "Yeah."

"Absolutely. But she didn't."

"What makes you so sure?" Davecki asked. He reclaimed his half step.

"She has a thing for guys in uniform. It's an authority issue. Some sort of fascination with powerful men or being overpowered. Her old man was a cop."

"Maybe that's motive enough," Davecki said.

"Not too likely," Breedy said and she flipped her hair back with her left hand. The hair on her right shoulder remained hanging in front.

"Why's that?"

"She always got what she wanted."

"From her dad or from Gronsby?"

"Both I suppose. But I meant Gronsby."

Davecki grabbed his chin. It was puzzlement time. "You ever been a cop?" he grinned.

Breedy wandered over to the other wall. She looked at another Jarvis photo. This one of a merganser taking off out of a splash of water. "I just read the papers and talk to people who come here." Her voice had become wistful.

"When did you last see Gronsby?"

Breedy turned away from the eight by twelve photo in its eleven by fourteen frame. "Last I know he was here two weeks ago. I was off that day. But Hazel mentioned it to me. She said Gronsby talked to Brooksie for a long time."

"Any idea what they talked about?"

"You don't really talk to dementia patients, you more or less just sit and listen and try to figure out if they're making sense or not. It takes a lot of time."

"Time you don't have with this place so full, right?"

Breedy looked sharply at Davecki. "I do my best."

"Which is very, very good I'm sure," Davecki said quickly. "Did Cheney say if Gronsby said anything that might have foreshadowed his demise?"

Breedy looked at him. "Foreshadowed his demise?'

Davecki felt himself blushing slightly. "I read alot."

"Right. You'll have to ask Hazi that. Thurber was

pretty much an open book as far as I'm concerned. He wanted to get those barrels raised. He hoped Brooksie would give him some solid evidence."

"That where he got the orange slime story?"

"I was with them when Brooksie brought it up. He has lucid moments...."

"Thurber?"

Breedy laughed. Davecki was glad she saw it as a joke.

"No, Brooksie. He has times when he'll be talking perfectly, like he's not at all demented. We were just sitting there and Brooksie's eyes changed. He sort of came alive and said, 'you can't make chicken salad out of chicken shit.' Thurber laughed and I said, 'what's that mean, Brooksie?' He said, 'Nuttin. It don't mean nuttin. I don't know nuttin at all 'bout no barrel leaking orange slime.'" Breedy was talking slang, imitating Brooks Robertson's speech Davecki presumed.

"Then what?" Davecki said.

"Well, Thurb asked Brooksie, 'What green slime?' 'It was orange,' Brooksie said. He was angry."

Davecki was tempted to ask, Gronsby or Brooks? but decided he'd been funny enough.

Breedy went on, "Brooksie started talking fast. He was obviously angry. He told a long story about how the crew was putting a barrel over the side. It slipped out of the barrel jack and fell. The lid flew off and there was a huge splash of orange slime. He said the deck hands just hosed the deck down and heaved the barrel over the gunnels."

Davecki grabbed his chin again. "So, that's where Gronsby got that information."

"He....Thurber," Breedy said looking shyly at Davecki, "asked Brooksie who the deckhands were. Brooks said, 'Knudson.' All he said was Knudson and the lights went out in his eyes," Breedy concluded. She looked sad to Davecki.

He reached into his shirt pocket and pulled the Lake Carrier's Association card from his pocket. "Would he have meant Lars Knudson?" Davecki said, extending the card toward Breedy.

She took the card and said sternly, "Where'd you get this? This is Brooksie's. His daughter accused us of stealing it from his personal effects."

"Gronsby had it on him when he died. It's evidence," Davecki said extending his hand again.

Breedy looked at him suspiciously and handed him the card.

"All righty then," the young man's voice came from behind the slowly opening door. A short, stocky guy with a dark mustache emerged from three twenty-six and said, "See yah, Captain Robertson." The man was folding a bundle of linen in on itself. "He's all yours," the man said looking at Breedy. He looked at Davecki and said, "This the C.G.A.?" The short guy looked Davecki up and down and said, "Not bad," and walked away.

"Don't mind Gary. He's a twerp," Breedy said. She walked into the dimly lit room without another word.

11

"Hello, Mr. Robertson," Breedy said loudly. "Someone wants to talk to you."

Davecki was shocked. Brooks Robertson was six foot ten and had to weigh two hundred and fifty pounds. For whatever reason, he was expecting a wizened old man that resembled the portrait of Captain McDougal that hung in the corner of the Hardees restaurant on Belknap. There was something awesome about the physical size of the guy. He must have been a mighty man in his day, Davecki thought.

"Captain Robertson," Davecki said extending his hand.

The big old guy on the bed sat up and grabbed the cop's hand. Davecki squeezed for everything he was worth and still the bones in his hand crunched and crackled like a car tire rolling over gravel.

"Nice to meet'cha," Robertson said letting go of the hand. "Sweetheart," Robertson said glancing over to Melody Breedy.

This guy seems normal, Davecki thought. He looked at Breedy. She smiled and shrugged her shoulders. Davecki looked back at Robertson and the man started singing. "Lake Superior, you know, doesn't give up her dead. It's a big lake they call Gitchi Gummi." Davecki saw in the man's eyes that the old salt was far, far away piloting a tug boat through a treacherous channel on the Detroit River or some such place.

"You know why your picture is on Lars Knudson's

LCA card?" Davecki asked holding the I.D. out.

"Card!" Robertson said snatching the plastic away.

Davecki quashed the urge to grab it back. A vision of the nightly news flashed into his mind. He saw video of his mug shot and taped segments of an enraged old giant of a man holding a dead detective in a head lock while battering a solid wall with abandon. The old man was holding the Association card to his lips, kissing it. Davecki looked at Breedy. She smiled some more. Davecki looked at Robertson. He smooched the card again and handed it back. Davecki took it. Robertson said, "Lars is dead. Lars is dead. The lake didn't get 'em. But the lake will glow. The lake will glow."

"What's that mean?" Davecki asked.

Robertson looked out his window. Outside, to the south, a big yard caressed two enormous willow trees directly in its middle. The wide green lawn, which was immaculately mown, sloped to the south for two acres. Beyond the yard was the ever present, thickly wooded, northern forest. Davecki looked at Breedy.

"Never been able to figure that one out," she said.

"Cappy," Davecki said pulling out his language from days long gone. "You know anyone who'd want to kill Thurber Gronsby?"

Breedy snorted.

Davecki felt anger rising alongside embarrassment.

"IBM! IBM!" Robertson chirped happily.

Davecki looked at Breedy. "Haven't a clue," she said, "maybe a bowel movement. Who knows?"

Something in the Water

Davecki was planning his getaway. He couldn't take the dissonance of a fully grown man with an apparently healthy body acting like a baby learning to talk. He was about to turn away when Robertson stopped grinning and cleared his throat. He sing songed, "I was seventeen going on eighteen. He was older. My card. My mug. His name. His dates. Together we faked 'dem jakes."

Davecki felt hot. One minute the guy's a nut, the next he's talking sense, he thought. He looked at Melody Breedy for support. She smiled and said, "That's the first time I heard that."

"The lake is gonna glow!" Robertson chanted.

"Like at sunset?" Davecki said recalling the tremendous visions of burning water he used to see at sunrise and sunset.

"Glow, glow don't-cha know," the seaman chanted. Then he moved back into the Fitz song, "Lake Superior you know don't give up her dead, glow, glow," he sang.

"We better go," Davecki said.

"See yah, Brooksie," Breedy said and started for the door. Davecki stepped back to let her pass. She stopped and knelt down to tie Robertson's shoes. As she crouched, Davecki saw her athletic haunches as her dress draped around the curve of her hips. He remembered his mother's preference for dresses and disdain for slacks.

After the shoe was over, after the knot, Breedy stood to leave. As she walked out, Davecki followed. Before he could get away, Robertson reached out and grabbed Davecki's arm. His voice shook. He said, "Gron-Gron says, watch out for IBM."

Out in the hallway, Davecki felt woozy. He groped for the handrail and used it as a guide while walking down the brightly lit Jarvis-decorated corridor. "I guess I'm going to have to pay Mr. Knudson a visit," he said.

"That's going to be a bit hard," Breedy said, "He died of cancer twelve years ago."

"Gronsby tell you that?"

"Yeah, he told me. All you cops think alike."

"I'm a detective."

"Not everyone can achieve the lofty position of detective?"

"Nor can just anyone acquire the enviable position of hanging around dead bodies and pursuing dead dock workers, and catching pipple who kill pipple....I'm the luckiest pipple in the world," Davecki said turning to the left, heading for the elevator.

"Who killed Thurber Gronsby?" Breedy asked.

Davecki punched the down button. There was no light to indicate the machine was coming up. Breedy leaned over, jabbed the button hard a couple of times and it lit up. "It's an old building," she said.

"This case might get to be old, too, if all my leads turn up dead or demented."

"It can't be that bad," Breedy said getting on the elevator.

"Oh?" Davecki said.

The door closed. Breedy turned to him. "Thurber wanted the barrels raised. Thurber's dead. He wasn't killed thirty years ago. He was killed last week."

Davecki felt hot again. He was acquiring a dislike for Lost Creek Nursing Home. "What's your point?"

"Somebody doesn't want those barrels raised, that person's alive today and dangerous enough to kill. Who could or would want to do that? It's simple."

Davecki was beginning to see his distaste had little to do with the home. "Of course it's simple. But it isn't easy. What would you do Miss Smarty Pants?"

"Smarty pants? That come from your vast reading?"

"It comes from growing up with sisters, all of whom, at the appropriate times, I administered suitable attitude adjustments to."

"Well, when it's appropriate, I can take an adjustment or two. Sorry." Breedy said as the doors opened.

"Apology accepted."

They walked toward the exit. Davecki was wondering what to do next. This quandary covered both the case and saying good-bye to Melody Breedy.

"What's up now? What's next?" she asked as she pushed open the doors in front of them.

They walked out into the marvelous June air. Davecki sniffed. Something smelled sweet. He looked around. Next to the entrance, on his right, was a well groomed flower bed. Davecki sniffed again. There were rows and banks of marigolds, zinnias and cosmos. "Kinda early for such great blossoms isn't it?" he asked.

Breedy chuckled and explained, "Mrs. Mellow

used to have championship flower gardens before coming here." She fidgeted.

Davecki said, "They're beautiful. He sniffed again and turned to examine the flower bed.

"You think some industrial conspiracy did Gronsby in?" Breedy asked. She didn't follow Davecki as he bent toward a clump of cosmos blossoms.

He sniffed again and said, "Not likely. I didn't think it was these. What in hell am I smelling?"

Breedy said, "Oh it's probably from the hayfield across the road."

"No way. I know that smell. I used to make hay for a farmer in Port Wing. Slaved all day just for a shot at his daughter in the hay mow," Davecki said absently as he vanished from Breedy's sight around the corner of the building.

Breedy didn't move. In about thirty seconds Davecki's voice echoed off the brick facade, "Oh Miss Breedy.... Would you please come here?"

Breedy lowered her head, shrugged her shoulders and walked around the corner. Davecki stood next to a tall green plant in the corner. "Mrs. Mellow **is** quite the gardener isn't she?" he said.

Breedy stammered, "It's... It's..." and she stared in silence for a second. Then her face changed, the confusion Davecki saw there vanished and she said, "Well, well. I will certainly have to tell Mrs. Mellow that she has completely overlooked a nasty weed of some type in her prize flower bed."

"Indeed, indeed," Davecki said.

They looked at each other for five full seconds. In

his earlier years, Davecki would have been grinning
for he would have attained some moral high ground
from which to plan the assault of immoral intentions
he would have had in mind for such a luscious lump
of femininity. But, now, today, in his middle age, all
he could think of was poor Mrs. Mellow desperately
in need of her medicinal marijuana and she so far from
Proposition 213 and California.

He sighed and let go of the pointy leaf he held
tenderly between his fingers. He put those same fingers to his nose and sniffed. "Nope. That's not it either," he said.

Breedy grinned.

He walked back to the front entrance and sniffed
a couple of times. They were exaggerated inhalations.
He swung his head all around like a bear trying to fix
the direction from which the honey scent was flowing.

Breedy, who had followed the cop to the sidewalk
between the entrance and the parking lot, laughed.

Davecki looked at her. She was smiling. She was
twinkling, not just in her eyes, but her whole aura
was sparkling like a giant diamond. Inside the black
half boots he wiggled his toes. Then it struck him.
He suddenly knew what the faint scent entering his
nose was and he knew exactly what to do next. Even
though he was fifteen miles away from it, Lake Superior was calling him, for the faint aroma he'd detected
was the unmistakable smell of fresh water in the distance.

"I'm going fishing," he said.

"I love to fish," Breedy said.

Davecki looked at her. He smiled and said, "Maybe someday. After the case is over, maybe."

Breedy smiled and looked up into the sky. She sniffed the air and said, "There's something about that water."

"There sure is," Davecki said and walked away smiling.

Neither of them said goodbye.

12

There's something about a pregnant woman, Davecki thought as he pulled his right foot out of the carburetor. Even though his Mustang was fuel injected, he liked the saying. Up ahead a half mile, he could see a female waddle, or at least what he suspected was a waddle, a pregnant waddle. His suspicions were what made him a good detective.

The speedometer needle lowered itself gently down past one hundred miles an hour. The back pressure on the exhaust rumbled. It was another thing he liked, speed in triple digits. He shifted to fourth gear and remembered the T-shirt he saw at the drag strip. **Life begins at 150** it said. He tried to buy one but couldn't find it anywhere.

With all the likeable things happening around him, Davecki couldn't figure out why he was so grumpy. He first noticed it in the parking lot of Lost Creek. No, it first happened when George Plimpton popped into the picture, it grew exponentially seeing a grown man like Robertson failing. Was he seeing his own future? The icky feeling compounded as he shifted down again and again, slowing to a stop next to the skinny backside of Theresa McGrath, soon-to-be mother Theresa McGrath.

Davecki powered down the rider's window and called out, "Hey Terry."

The beautiful young face that turned to greet him was tear stained and reddened. It also sported the beginnings of a shiner. She put a hand up to cover her eye. And through it all, damn it, Davecki thought, she was still beautiful. "Get in," Davecki commanded.

The girl wedged herself into the passenger's space. Davecki's stomach grabbed at his backbone with both hands and started doing the hokey pokey. Then it stuck its right foot in and shook it all about. "Where is he?"

Theresa, between her sobs said, "He said he was going to the Choo Choo." The Choo Choo bar was another of Superior's more funky locations. It was in the cars of an old railroad train and it was located right across the highway from where Theresa and George both worked.

Davecki put the Stang in gear and didn't ignite the tires. He was so angry he was tempted to burn-out mightily, but he refrained from expressing the full extent of his wrath in deference to the wounded woman next to him. She'd had enough machismo for one day. The car sped up as she gently wept. "I'm taking you to the shelter," he announced.

"No," she said.

"Yes," he countered.

"Please don't. I just want to go home."

Davecki looked at the girl. She had black hair. Beautiful thick eyebrows arched above the deep brown eyes. He wondered what color Melody Breedy's eyes were. Theresa's nose was starting to swell from the blow. Had she not been involved with Mr. Wrong, it would have been a cute little pug nose affair that turned up slightly at the tip. Her lips were curvaceous and her chin repeated the graceful line of her nose.

"Home as in your house or home as in Lost Creek?" Davecki asked.

Something in the Water

Theresa turned and looked at the cop. She winced from the movement. "Mama told me not to accept rides from strange men," she laughed.

"That's strangers, Terry."

They laughed.

"I could take you to your mom's."

Theresa laughed.

It was, to Davecki, a bad sign.

"Dad's a drunk fisherman in Alaska, remember? And Ma's living with a quantum traveling, lithium saturated school teacher from Proctor." she said.

Davecki didn't remember the drunk part. "So it's the shelter then?"

Theresa shook her head no, but only briefly as the pain stopped her. "No. Home-home. The trailer," she said.

"I'm taking you to emergency," Davecki said. "You're hurt."

"Home-home, officer," she said without looking away from the road ahead.

Davecki admired her strong will. She was a fool, but a determined fool would survive, and thrive eventually. Then he was grateful that Plimpton had chosen to pound the right side of her face. That way the view from the driver's side seemed normal. And that's how Theresa wanted to play it, as if it was nothing unusual to be unmarried, pregnant, and hiking down a lonely highway with your face smashed in. There was no elephant shit in her living room.

"Turn here," she said.

Davecki took a right onto Rockmount Road and

drove beyond the woods to a driveway on the left. Out in the middle of a hayfield stood a trailer, a small trailer with no skirting. Davecki knew it still wouldn't have skirting in January and all of Theresa's tip money would be going for fuel oil just to keep the baby warm. Thank God for WIC he said to himself and made a commitment to stop often and tip large at the Town Lier restaurant where she worked. He stopped a few feet from the trailer's door and decided it was more of a camper.

"It's Dad's fifth-wheeler," she said as if she'd read his mind.

Davecki was about to say, "Uh-hum."

She kept talking, "He's not that bad," she said.

"Your Dad or George?"

She laughed. "Both, really," she said, "But I was talking about Dad for some reason. Oh yeah. The camper. He let us take it for as long as we need to get on our feet."

Davecki looked around. An old car engine without the added blessing of a car in sight, sat on the grass ten yards to his left. A couple of faux wire wheel hubcaps, some old two by fours, an old tire without a wheel and an old mattress cluttered the yard. It wasn't really a yard it was a hayfield where the farmer had just cut first crop hay a few weeks, or days, earlier. He wondered, who let them park here?

"My Aunt Phoebe let us park here."

It was Davecki's turn to look at her sharply.

"You're like an open book," she said.

Davecki felt a chill run up his spine. Goose bumps

rose on both his arms despite it being seventy degrees in the shade. She just stared at him. As he looked at her, he felt as if he was ten miles from her and an inch from her nose at the same time. He had to look away. Through the bug-gut-smeared windshield he saw a gray horse walk out from behind the camper. Davecki noticed the electric fence now.

"That's my horse, Piglet," Theresa announced. "You wanna meet him?"

Anything to get her off my wavelength, Davecki thought as he quickly reached for his door-latch. He was afraid he might think something sexy and she'd say something and.....

Theresa laughed.

Davecki practically jerked the latch off the door he wanted out so bad.

They walked up to the horse. It nickered gently. Theresa put out her hand. The horse flapped its nose and nickered again.

"No, no carrot," she said. Theresa moved in closer and put her hand on the animal's neck. The horse moved it's nose up to Theresa's right eye and snorted.

"Of course it was George. Officer Davecki doesn't want to **hit** me," she said.

The horse nickered and tossed its head.

"Yeah I think that's probably true," she said. She turned her gaze from the horse to Davecki and smiled. It was shy and sad at the same time.

"It's Detective," he said and turned to leave. He couldn't take it a second longer.

"Relax Dave," Theresa said, "I'm not going to hurt you."

"No shit," Davecki said. "But you're spooking me out. And I've got to get to the Choo Choo and make an arrest."

"Don't waste your time on him. Leave him to me. You need to get to your fishing."

"How'd you know I was going fishing?"

"You mentioned it didn't you?" she said patting the horse on the nose.

"No I did not. At least I don't remember saying anything."

"I'm sure you did. Something about your friend John calling you to go fishing."

The second Theresa stopped talking, Davecki's phone chirped in his pocket.

Fucking-A, he thought as he reached for the cellular. He pulled it and walked away. Any distance from this chick was better than none. He stood by the Stang and listened to John Chuckson explain that the day's charter had limited out early. That he'd be at the Barker's Island charter deck in twenty minutes if he wanted to head back out to murder some more fishies.

Davecki was in shock. He realized he was not only outstanding in his field but standing out in a farmer's field listening to his friend whisper in his ear while that very friend was twenty miles away and on a fishing boat. He was watching a young, pregnant woman whispering things in a horse's ear and that she would probably name the baby, Damien. It would grow up to be the anti-Christ and that Alphonse "Dave" Davecki would go down in history as the one guy who had a chance to kill the anti-Christ while standing in the poor white trash yard where the Evil One, the Great Anti-Christ was born and raised by a talking horse who wasn't Mr. Ed.

Davecki realized too, when he heard Chuckson's voice repeating itself in his ear, "Dave? Dave? You there? You going to meet me?" that he was losing it.

"Yeah," Davecki said, "I'll be there," and he hung up his phone fast because Theresa had let the horse out of the fence and they were walking over to him.

"Piglet says you really, really, need to go fishing," Theresa said.

"That's my plan," Davecki said. Theresa chuckled and the horse threw its head up and down enjoying the joke, whatever it was.

"Before you go Dave, there's something you should know."

Davecki opened the Stang's door and propped himself between it and them. He didn't say anything, but he was waiting, not fleeing.

"Dad was a longshoreman. He worked with Gramps on the barrel project when they dumped 'em in the water. Thurber Gronsby talked to Dad a lot about what happened back then, how they dumped 'em, where. All that stuff."

Davecki was grateful she was talking normal. Piglet tossed his head. "So your father corroborated the orange goo?"

"Yeah, he told Gronsby everything. Everything Gronsby knew about the barrels he got from Dad and Grandad."

Maybe your old man isn't really in Alaska, Davecki thought.

"Dad didn't kill Gronsby," Theresa said. "If anyone killed him it was Dominick Navarone."

Davecki sighed. Shit, he thought, this case was getting more constipated all the time.

"It's not that hard," Theresa said.

Or, Davecki wondered, was it the horse that spoke? Or were they even speaking? Maybe this was a dream. Who knew? It was all too freaky. "Things can be simple, but usually they're hard," Davecki said and cared not a whit that he was thinking dirty all of a sudden.

"Now you're getting it Detective. You got to pretend it's October. You've got to take the world less seriously."

Resisting the urge to punch her himself, Davecki smiled and knew he wouldn't cold-cock George Plimpton the next time they met.

"What's Navarone got to do with this?"

"Other than killing Thurber Gronsby, everything," Theresa said. As she spoke, the sound of a car coming down the road emerged from the tree-line at the edge of the field. All three of them looked west to see a black Pontiac 6000 zooming down the gravel road. Steam billowed from under the hood.

"Shit," Davecki said, "Now I've got to arrest him."

"No you don't. Let me handle him," Theresa said.

"It's against the law to let him go."

"It's against the law to drive one hundred and thirty miles an hour on country roads," she said.

Davecki felt boxed in. He watched as the Pontiac slowed for the driveway, actually it was just the field crossing where the tractors entered and exited the acreage. Then it was obvious that Plimpton had seen the Mustang because the car sped up and vanished over the hill toward highway 53. Davecki was going to call the state patrol. They could make the pinch if they were close.

"He won't be able to work if he's in jail."

"There's always the Huber Law," Davecki said.

"Then he's in the slammer every night and I'm all alone out here in this shack." Such a possibility actually appealed to him. The horse snorted. It's eyes got bigger and Davecki suddenly laughed. The utter safeness of the child and her horse struck him solidly in the solar plexus and he remembered the C.S. Lewis book of a similar name. Theresa laughed explosively and held her hand to her mouth. Little rivulets of silvery drool ran down her fingers.

"I gotta go," Davecki said. He slid into his car and left the clairvoyant and her horse behind. Ahead he had fishing, a trip to Red Cliff and some research on the rich union boss, Nick Navarone. Behind him, far behind him is where he wanted to leave Terry McGrath's attractive saliva and her horse.

She put her hand to the horse's mouth. A broad pink tongue swiped at her fingers. "Bye Dave," she said.

He said nothing and backed around, being careful not to ram the 350 engine block laying on its side in the hay stubble, being careful not to project his own conviction that he wasn't really leaving, he was fleeing. In the rear view mirror he saw the horse's lips moving and couldn't say for sure, but could have sworn he heard a deep resonant, "It was delightful Detective," in his ear. The voice reminded him of his father's.

13

Davecki pointed the Mustang right on Rockmont, but not before looking left. He mourned the loss of a high speed chase with Plimpton. His grief wasn't so much about the escape of a law breaker, it was something else. As he drove, the dismayed detective tried to inventory his anxiety.

The Mustang, good little pony that it was, seemed to be finding its own way home. Instead of Sam Anderson Hill, it chose the long, but blacktop, way around the knob of basalt that contained at least two quarries, a gravel pit and one old gold mine. As the highway curved around the hill, it brought the car up and over a crest, the land fell away dramatically and opened up a majestic view to the north. Davecki let the sixty miles of openness between his nose and the North Shore please him. He felt the solace of wide open spaces crunch the crystallized stress in his chest into a virtually non-existent powder. The great expanse of green forest spread across the wide rift valley for ten miles. The view was as spectacular as any out of Africa. Davecki had always wanted to go to Africa. His first desires for the Dark Continent began with National Geographic. It was fourth grade. Ray Pozzi, Tommy Ludak, Jeff Jones, Dennis Hipsher and he gathered around the yellow bordered book for long looks at the black breasts therein. Back then, he just stared. He grew into wanting to touch. When he turned forty-six, he realized it wasn't lust but grief that drove him so. That awareness calmed his greed greatly and he started looking around for alternatives to female solace.

One of the consolations was the Big Lake and the beauty of the place in which he lived. The view across the last miles of Wisconsin was majestic and Davecki knew he'd contented himself with home, that he'd never see Africa and that was fine. Sad, but fine.

Also fine was the sight of Lake Superior. It reminded him of seeing the Yukon River. He was covering the Iditarod for the Alaska Radio Network, flying with a bush pilot friend from Anchorage to Nome. The Yukon rose out of the forest like a monster snake. Its immensity dominated the geography like King Kong in New York City. Lake Superior was a Godzilla-like piece of work too. It commanded respect. It snowed the south shore in. It sank eight hundred foot ships. It provided drinking water for millions and diluted the waste from them all. It drank twenty-nine sailors in one gulp. It bent the earth's crust with its weight. It made love to all who lived near it. It pissed its lovers off with its fickleness. And, Davecki knew as the sight of the lake vanished behind the trees between the freeway and the county highway, it was calling to him now. He wanted to go fishing badly.

The Stang wanted to get off the two-lane. Badly or not, Davecki didn't know, but he found himself choosing, uncharacteristically, to take the freeway into town. As the car turned right just past Country Boy Auto Wrecking, Davecki found another source of anxiety within.

What was he doing? He felt stupid. The investigation was a complete monkey fuck. Nothing made sense. Gronsby was dead and nobody knew why. Nobody seemed to have a motive. There were plenty of suspects, but they were all weak, Hazel Cheney was capable but unlikely. Nick Navarone was capable but improbable. Why would a rich Minnesota ex-union boss jeopardize his fortune and freedom? The Indian thing was a mixture of ancient hostility and jealousy that amounted to grasping at straws. Sure Gronsby was wrapped up in a gill net, but those nets were free-floating all over the lake these days. Brooks Robertson didn't have the opportunity.

Nothing made sense to Davecki. He discovered he had a death grip on the leather covered steering wheel when his thinking got to Robertson. He couldn't figure out the old man's disjointed statements. The lake glowing he could accept. Sunrise, sunset, quickly through the years; all that. But the IBM comment. It was so out of whack. Probably he'd mixed up Honeywell and IBM. That had to be it. Honeywell dumped the barrels not IBM.

Davecki let go of the steering wheel completely. The car stayed straight and true. It didn't pull left or wander right. He loved new tires. He was happy for Duluth Tire, that he could buy great tires cheap. He wanted something to be happy about. He learned in four and a half decades that it was his responsibility to focus on the happy stuff. "Good things can happen as well as bad," Davecki said out loud and he thumped the steering wheel twice.

The three tower array of radio antennas on the

left side of the highway glided past. Ever since he was a kid, he loved to watch those imposing towers glide by. They were one reason he went into radio. Were they moving? Or he? He wondered why those towers always fascinated him. His venture in broadcasting only lasted a few years but did teach him that the booth was too confining. Plus, the pay sucked. But still, there was always something magical to him about talking into a mic in an isolation chamber in some building and being heard by millions. The *calling-out-from-within-the-deep-chamber-thing* was always a mystic/symbolic/cosmic thing for Davecki. He wished he'd studied Hinduism more in college. He might have a better word for it than thing.

One thing he knew, he'd better slow down, Davecki thought as he ripped by the state patrol's speed trap between Highway Thirteen and Moccasin Mike Road. His speedometer read eighty-two. Even the fact that he was a cop wouldn't get him out of a ticket for that speed and he was grateful the trooper was occupied elsewhere. He retracted his right foot and let compression braking slow him.

The edge of town rose from the earth like opening a gigantic pop-up card. He shifted to fourth to make forty miles an hour. He slowed even further when an enormous purple Western Star pulp truck pulled out in front of him as it left the Holiday station on the right. The truck's door had "Tim Martens" painted on it. The truck pulled a single axle pup trailer that reminded Davecki of a little baby truck following its mama like a duckling.

Something in the Water

The next thing Davecki knew he was walking down C-dock at Barker's Island Marina. Happy fisherpeople were walking toward him clutching pink salmon and yellow trout fillets in Ziploc bags. Chuckson had added yet another six people to his already long list of satisfied customers.

"Hey Dave," Chuckson said as the cop walked up. The Wonder-Swede was cranking on the spigot of the water hose next to the shore-power on the dock.

"John," Davecki said.

"I'll be ready to cast off in a second," Chuckson said as he hosed blood and fish guts off his fillet board. The slender fillet knife was already cleaned and glistening on the dock. Davecki went aboard the Formula, felt the familiar rocking of the seaworthy vessel, ducked into the cabin and took off his bomber. He knew he'd put it back on soon, but he wanted out of his shoulder holster. He could never figure out why normal people would allow some people to walk around heavily armed. It was okay as long as he was the one with the gun. Davecki tucked the weapon into the corner of the seat by the lower controls. He hunched his shoulders and cracked his clavicles like an eighth grader cracking his knuckles.

The boat rocked to the starboard. Captain John was aboard. "I'll fire her up. You grab the bow line," the voice came down from the flying bridge. Davecki re-donned his jacket and thought of Joe Don Baker. Davecki thought of the Mark Twain line, "The coldest winter I ever spent was a summer in Duluth."

"Where's Willow today?" he asked emerging from his changing room.

"She's decorating some fancy room in the Manson Mansion. Hog heaven for her," Chuckson answered before twisting the twin keys that ignited the dual engines below deck.

Davecki unwrapped the line from the cleat and twirled it over the bow rail. He walked back to the stern line, untied it and tossed it aboard as the Merc-Cruiser clunked into gear. Davecki jumped across the widening gap between the dock and boat. Five baby mallards paddled away from the transom in dark water made turbulent by the twin jet-props that Chuckson had personally self-hammered for maximum efficiency. There was one thing John Chuckson was obsessive about, his boat and fishing. Okay that's two, Davecki laughed to himself and knew that as long as he lived, if his mind didn't go south like Robertson's, he'd never be bored for long.

Davecki joined Chuckson on the flying bridge. The boat glided past the "no wake" buoy which leaned its white and red body away from the encroaching Bertram. "Any luck with the Gronsby thing?"

Davecki harumphed and said, "Unless you call meeting a weird mind-reading chick, lucky."

"Nice rack?"

"Naw, poor skinny little pregnant thing."

"Lucky you," Chuckson said and he pushed both throttles forward with the sure hand of a many seasoned veteran fisherman.

The boat sped past the last No Wake buoy into Superior Bay. The men sat together in silence. It was a grand tradition. Get on board, get under-way and shut up. Davecki recalled the Sturgis t-shirt. It said, "Get on. Hang on. Shut up." What could be more satisfying? The water was blue. The sky the same. Puffball clouds hung above them. On the right, the Old Great Northern Dock brooded silently about its abandonment. The Burlington Docks came alongside. The Roger Blough lounged on the waters of Allouez Bay, gulping in pellets fed from the multiple conveyor belts of BN Taconite. The Blough was eight hundred and fifty eight feet long and one hundred and five feet wide. It reminded Davecki of a lazy cat stretched out in the sun on a cozy blue carpet. The Blough was designed by Marine Consultants and Designers, Inc. and built by The American Ship Building Company. It was one of the last good looking ships built for the taconite trade. All the new vessels were basically barges, big scows designed to move the most bulk cargo in the most efficient manner. Beauty be damned. Davecki was thankful it didn't look like the Stewart Cort or the Belle River. Over the roar of the wind he shouted to Chuckson, "It's too bad they don't build ships like the Ford or the Ryerson." He pointed at the Blough.

"What?" Chuckson yelled.

"Nothing," He answered.

Davecki envisioned the E.M. Ford. He could practically see the stubby little ship with its graceful lines from a bygone era. Built in 1898 at Cleveland Ship Building Company in Lorain, Ohio, it was the oldest ship still operating on the lakes and classic in styling. Though it was shortened radically to make it better able to haul cement, the ship was beautiful in an elegant way. Plus, it cradled an antique quadruple expansion steam engine in its hull, adding to its mystique. The vision of the Ford vanished and the Blough regained its claim on Davecki's reality. He recalled Roger Blough, Chairman of U.S. Steel, taking on President Kennedy. Maybe Oswald did a good thing, Davecki thought and felt deeply ashamed.

As the twin Chevy engines powered them at thirty-two miles an hour out of the Wisconsin Entry, Davecki looked down the long strand of beach that was Wisconsin Point. He shuddered. A week ago he was over there staring at the gray and lamprey marked face of Thurber Gronsby. Nothing really good had happened since. The air blew past Davecki's face as they broke into open water past the lighthouse. Chuckson pushed the chrome throttle handles further forward and yelled above the whipping wind and roaring engines, "Take'r to Lester. I'm going below to rig a rod."

The captain vanished down the ladder and Davecki grabbed the wheel. He looked at the compass mounted on the dash and decided to hold her where she sat on twenty-three degrees. If that heading didn't lead to the Lester River, and if Chuckson stayed below too long, he could make corrections later when they got closer to the boats dotting the horizon.

The drone of the engines and the wash of fresh Lake Superior air hypnotized and cleansed Davecki's over-active mind. The boat surged over gentle one foot rollers. The sensation was one of rhythmic rocking under the administration of reliable power. It occurred to Davecki that it didn't matter if nothing good had happened regarding the case.

The next thing he knew Chuckson was beside him yelling. "Bring her around to the west and start heading back toward the bridge. I'll start throwing lines." Chuckson dropped out of sight to the lower deck and Davecki hauled the wheel left. He pulled back on the throttles and the boat stopped its forward progress like it had been tackled by Reggie White.

"Use the port engine," Chuckson yelled. "It's idling better. The starboard needs new points."

Davecki turned the starboard key to vertical and half the engine noise behind him vanished. The other half of the internal combustion duo below deck continued to purr as the backwash from Formula's wake caught and tossed the boat. Davecki felt comforted by another fact, the fact that there were still engines around that used points and condensers and weren't fuel injected. He felt a kinship to carburetors wash across his soul and sneered inwardly at computer chip controlled engines that couldn't be repaired for less than two hundred dollars if the brain box puked. Davecki needed simple right now, needed to put the complexity of the case behind him.

"What's the depth?" Chuckson asked.

Davecki looked at the depth finder and answered, "Ninety."

Chuckson replied, "They've been hitting all day on Fedo Flyers and Meronek Moonshiners with flashers at forty feet. Nudge that throttle up a C.H." He was attaching a little fish-like lure to a line.

Davecki bumped the bottom of the throttle knob with the heel of his hand and listened for the subtle change in sound that signaled a slight increase in RPMs. He watched the depth finder report the speed increase. The sun warmed his back. He stared blankly at the green shoreline of East Duluth. He stopped thinking. The white hot blaze of his stressful focus on the case cooled.

Before long, Chuckson had the outriggers deployed. He'd played out lines to the sides and was now rigging a twelve pound depth bomb. The competent captain worked the Canon downrigger toggle with his left hand. With his right he whipped long lengths of line off the Garcia reel as the equipment operated perfectly.

"Here fishy, fishy, fishy..." Davecki called out across the water.

"If you fish it, they will come," Chuckson said. He tightened the drag on the reel and clambered up to the bridge. "All set," he announced.

"Now to slay 'em," Davecki said.

"Not a problem."

The men motored along at trolling speed and fell into the pattern of circling that the five other hulls in the vicinity were doing. It was an unorchestrated, unchoreographed dance that all the charter boats do. In the distance, about a mile off to the southeast, a seven hundred foot saltie was at anchor. After a while of watching lines, Davecki noticed one boat in the distance that wasn't operating like the others. "What's the deal there? Davecki asked pointing northeast.

Something in the Water

"Oh that Bayliner? That's the ragheads on IBM," Chuckson said easily.

Davecki's gut clenched. Chuckson returned his focus to the depth finder screen. "They may be a bit deeper this late in the day," Chuckson added. "I'm going to lower the downriggers. Take the helm," he said.

Davecki barely heard him for the Gronsby case had once again inflamed his brain.

14

"What did you say?" Davecki yelled after the descending fisherman.

Chuckson looked up from the lower deck, surprise on his face. "Lighten up, Dave. It's just a bunch of know-nothing foreigners trying to catch fish without the services of a highly trained charter captain."

"No way," Davecki said firmly. "Where's your binocs?" he added and turned toward the white dot on the horizon about a half mile of the starboard quarter at forty degrees on the compass.

"Don't turn so sharp! You'll foul the lines," Captain John yelled from the stern.

Davecki cut the wheel back ten degrees.

"The binocs are broke. Willow took 'em to First Photo to get fixed."

"We're going to have to get close then," Davecki said. He was happy all of a sudden. This new info meant he didn't have to go to Red Cliff.

Chuckson finished lowering the down-riggers and was reeling side lines for down planers when Davecki decided to tell him about Robertson's comment concerning IBM. He left the helm and was lowering himself down the ladder when Chuckson's yelp of, "FISH ON!" echoed in his ears.

Davecki's gut seized again. Captain John had the pole from the starboard down-rigger in his hands. He took in the slack, cranking the handle of the Garcia reel tenderly while holding the pole away from his body as the rod tip lowered. Then in an instant, he hauled back on the rod sharply and continued reeling. He reeled the arch of fiberglass back down toward the water's surface and then held it out to Davecki. "You land it. I'll get the net."

Davecki took the rig and kept cranking. "Feels like a lunker," he said as he hauled back on the line.

"Could be. Got a ton of line out for depth though," Chuckson said as he fetched the long handled net from the boat's port side. Chuckson put the net down, hanging the scoop over the transom. The butt of the handle stuck halfway back to the cabin door. "Captain Chuck is still good luck!" he called out in a singsong voice. He ducked into the cabin to make a steering correction. "Keep 'em coming, steady now," Chuckson said.

"It's coming in hard," Davecki said. Drops of sweat formed on his temples. He reeled the tip down and started hauling up with his left hand. He let go of the crank and shrugged out of the right arm of his bomber. Then he grabbed the rod with his right hand, kept pulling up and flipped off the left jacket sleeve. He shrugged the garment to the top of the engine compartment hood and resumed cranking.

Chuckson threw the jacket into the cabin below and picked up the net. "What's so interesting about the Bayliner?" Chuckson said.

"All of a sudden they're suspects in the Gronsby murder," Davecki said, still twisting line onto the spool.

"Hot damn," Chuckson said. "We're going to end up pretty close to them," he said peering around the cabin and across the Bertram's bow.

"Good," Davecki said.

"Keep that tip up," Chuckson advised.

"Up yours," Davecki said. "He's close."

Suddenly, about twenty-five yards across the water, a giant silver fish leapt from the water and flashed brilliantly in the sunlight. "Hot damn!" Chuckson said.

"Hot damn, yourself," Davecki shouted.

"That's twenty pounds if an ounce!" the charter captain yelled.

"Don't screw up netting it." Davecki shouted. Sweat was on his forehead now.

"All you worry about is getting it close, Davecki."

The fish, getting a shorter and shorter leash all the time, decided to go acrobatic again. It flung itself out of the blue water like a silver bullet and shot back down in a sparkling splash.

"That's a silver," Chuckson said.

"They don't get that big! Davecki countered.

"This one does," the captain grinned.

"This fish does not want to stop swimming," Davecki said hauling back on the rod and holding the crank steady. Line ran backwards out of the reel. "Should I set the drag up?"

"No way. It'll just break the line. Take it easy we're not going anywhere fast," Chuckson said watching in fascination as the fish ripped line off the reel. The despooling line hummed aloud, hissed through the eyelets. The line going out so fast created a time-standing-still kind of hypnotic state in Davecki. He listened and watched the reel as he stood motionless and the fish, far away and in another world altogether, expressed a will contrary to Davecki's. The trance seemed to last forever, at least until something began to intrude. It was a faint popping sound like firecrackers going off in the distance. Then there were splashes in the water, little ones.

"What the hell?" Chuckson said looking over his shoulder. "Holy shit," he said dropping the net as he dove for the cutty cabin.

"What?" Davecki said, alarmed at the captain's abandoning of the net. Chuckson would never abandon such a fish. Davecki struggled to turn around. They were about to broadside the IBM! Chuckson was diving for the helm to avoid the collision.

Despite the danger, Davecki didn't want to let the fish go. He could lock the reel, put the rod in a holder and risk letting the fish snap the line. That was something he most certainly didn't want to do. He'd never caught a twenty pound silver before. Besides, there was nothing he could do to help Chuckson, the best power boat captain in the harbor, avoid the crash.

However, he changed his mind when he too figured out what the popping noises were, which explained the numerous little geysers erupting all around them. They were being shot at!

Davecki flipped the reel's lock lever into position and holstered the rod. "Don't leave me fishy," he prayed aloud as he rushed into the cabin for his Glock. Chuckson's big body filled the pilot's seat utterly. "They're shooting at us!" he said whipping the helm hard to port.

"This I know, John," Davecki said calmly. "That's

why I'm trying to get my gun," he added as he reached around the big guy's legs. Davecki was amused as the wish entered his mind. Only he could be getting shot at and be wishing another man's wife were piloting the boat at this moment. Maybe a stray bullet will pop me in the head and give me the lobotomy I need, he thought as he grabbed his gun and ran for the after deck. Emerging from the cabin he thought of that poor Kennedy daughter being lobotomized by her loving father Joe and banished to Wisconsin.

Out in the air, the first thing Davecki noticed was the change in lighting. He hadn't noted it before but, clouds had rolled in, or something like clouds, for the sunny day had suddenly turned dark and creepy. He shivered. Something about the rapid weather change was spooky. He was accustomed to rapid weather changes in the Twin Ports, but this was unnatural, unsettling. Fog was rapidly engulfing the boats. Another retort from the gun on the deck of the IBM snapped him out of his trance.

"Halt! Police!" he yelled into the growing gloom.

"What the hell's going on?" Chuckson's voice echoed out of the cabin.

"Allah, Allah. Awkmalla Allah Balla," Davecki heard a distinctly Middle Eastern voice calling from the deepening shadows.

Then the two boats collided.

Davecki, standing in his ready-to-fire stance, was completely unprepared for the jolt. He tried to save himself but the impact knocked him into the gunwale and overboard. Of course, as he fell he tried to grab the edge of the Formula. This meant, of course, that he let go of the Glock. He heard it splash into the water a second before he felt the icy grip of the Big Lake embrace him with her utterly shocking arms.

Davecki surfaced, gasping for air. Actually he wasn't technically gasping. His mouth was agape. There was air poised to be drawn into his flabbergasted lungs. But nothing was happening. His entire being had been rudely put on hold by the water's cold cuddle. He now understood rapid immersion syndrome and why Baptists were tough folk, for, even though he desperately wanted to inhale, he could not breathe. His chest muscles were paralyzed. His mouth stood open. It was ready to receive oxygen, but his solar plexus, totally pissed off at the cold embrace, refused to cooperate. Then something clicked inside him and he took a breath. Never was air so welcome.

The upward motion of his first panicked kicking had popped him to the surface of the water quickly. He dunked under again just in time to see a phantom individual through the growing gloom. This individual was not Captain Chuck. This individual was not standing on the deck of the Formula. This individual was extremely swarthy and this individual was pointing a gun at him. As Davecki sank, he heard and felt the water above him explode. He saw a 9 mm slug drift down past him. He tried to stay submerged. Alas, he could not stay under long. He seemed to be remarkably buoyant and still, there was something about air his lungs craved. When he surfaced he couldn't see anything.

Mike Savage

Now, on Lake Superior there is fog, fog and fog. The first fog is a friendly mist that makes nearby objects seem soft and touchable. The second fog requires lights for driving, caution and slow speeds. Then there's spooky, end-of-the-world **FOG**. This **FOG** is so thick it deadens sound, disorients you while you're standing still and makes the blackness of midnight on a cloudy, moonless night seem like high noon on the equator.

To this **FOG**, Davecki surfaced and he instantly knew he was in deep do-do for he could see absolutely nothing. Compounding his fear was his sense that this particular fog was evil —or at least really, really pissed off— and that it was coming directly out of the lake in which he was treading water. And he hated Peter Benchley. Why? Because, as unreasonable as it was, in that water, in that **FOG**, feeling fear grow exponentially in his gut, Davecki saw as clearly as he envisioned the form and function of the E.M. Ford, a gigantic white shark shooting up from the depths of the water below him. The shark's mouth was gaping and ready to devour him. Being a basically prudent man, he did what comes naturally to prudent men. "Our Father, who art in heaven," he started praying out loud. "Please lend me a hand here."

15

The **FOG** as Davecki's mother used to say was, "sicker n' sea poop." As he concentrated on breathing, the doused detective found yet another surprise inside him. He was continually surprised by himself, endlessly fascinated with the variety of responses he was capable of and —at this particular moment— intensely devoted to himself. So it came as a shock to Davecki that he was not afraid to die.

He could not see an inch. *Maybe Ma really did mean, "See poop,"* he thought as he struggled to swim. The **FOG** was spectacularly spooky. Even though he was utterly wet, he could still feel the mist —or was it myst?— on his face. He remembered the Eskimo man in Unalakleet, Alaska explaining why he wasn't cold and why Davecki, who was covering the Iditarod for the Alaskan Radio Network, was shivering to death. "Me all face," Clarence Irigoo explained.

Funny what you think about when you're about to drown, Davecki thought. What did Thurber Gronsby think about? Was he cold? Did his mother come to mind? His father or some kindly Eskimo man? What about those lamprey? How did they get ahold of Gronsby's face? Where did the net come from? Did chocolate grow on trees in heaven?

Davecki shook his head at that last thought. He was going crazy. Was he going crazy? Why was this dream so weird? Okay now, it's time to wake up, he thought. It's so cold. So wet. Did I fall asleep in the tub? Why had the bath water gotten so cold? Why can't I wake up? Why are my arms so tired? Where are my legs? What's going on?

Then his hand hit something. It was solid. He swept his arm back in the same direction, such as direction was in this dream, he commented to himself. As his hand moved back toward the object he'd touched, he seemed to remember Captain Chuck being in this dream. Where had he gone?

Then his hand struck the object again. He grabbed it and pulled. His body followed his arm. He remembered the movie THX-1138. It was George Lucas' first film. It was science fiction. About the future on earth. The heroes tried to escape the evil city. They smashed a car and were arrested. They awoke in a fog. They were warm, safe and fed. But, they were completely befuddled about direction or location. It was a jail-fog. There were other people present and everyone talked about the impossiblity of escape. Davecki was glad for the hero of that movie because he didn't believe the others and started walking in what he considered a straight line. It was a courageous act of faith which was eventually rewarded when the hero bumped his nose directly and painfully into a white wall. Then he was faced with another impossibility. The wall seemed seamless and endless. But he kept searching. Eventually, he found a door, opened it, and stepped out of the fog back into reality.

Davecki's nose smacked into something hard. "Ouch!" he cried.

"Dave?!" he heard Chuckson's voice reverberate through the myst/mist.

Something in the Water

"In shawla dumb doobie dam camcorder." Another high pitched, more panicked voice replied.

Davecki pulled his aching nose higher and away from what ever he'd struck and found some purchase with his knees. He was, by instinct, pulling himself out of the water and onto something. It felt like the diving platform on the Formula. As he flopped out of the water, he wondered if his salmon was still hooked. He wanted to call out to Chuckson but didn't because he could see something that made him very nervous.

It was writing on the wall. He recalled Daniel and King Nebuchanezzer and he put his face right up next to the wall and moved it along. It made him cross-eyed to be so close, but he followed along, just like in the blackboard in Mrs. Meronek's second grade class. "Follow along on the board, class!" he could still hear his beloved teacher saying. The first word he discerned was, Inshalah. The second was, Bachrah. The third was, Malesh.

Damn! Davecki thought. IBM. He was aboard the raghead boat. It wasn't a dream. He _was_ going to die. All this time he thought he would leave this world in a _Death by Corvette,_ but here he was, about to be shot from above like a sixty inch muskie by some insane Hadji who couldn't take a little ramming accident with a grain of salt. Sheesh!

One thing changed in Davecki's new paradigm. He was suddenly grateful for the **FOG**. If he couldn't see beyond the transom, the enemy couldn't see either. He got to his knees and searched around the top of the transom with his hands. First he found a downrigger mount. He pulled himself up and kept feeling the Bayliner's curves. Next he touched the gasoline filler cover-plate. Then he touched a .....goddamn Saddam.... a hand!

A bulk freighter full of shrieking erupted as Davecki grabbed the digits like Gidget clutching cash and reefed with all his might. The screeching ended in a splash.

Gunfire erupted.

"God dammit," Davecki heard Chuckson's voice cursing into, or through, or around the **FOG**.

"Shibboleth antilla kamchatka consume repitour," Davecki heard as he swung himself aboard the boat. No way was he going to speak and reveal his position. He really wanted to ask what was happening to Chuckson with the gunfire and the cursing and all. He sat there three seconds waiting for an answer to his prayer. "The bastards shot Yosemite!" Chuckson's voice rang out.

So he was shot in the right shoulder, Davecki thought recalling John's Yosemite Sam tattoo.

"Hemoglobin Allah ma Gawbee, a disembodied voice echoed.

"Done done me wrong homo sapien," Chuckson's voice resounded.

Davecki turned his head trying to discern where the people connected to the voices might be. He felt like an owl rotating its head for mouse sounds. Chuckson's detatched words, "Take this! You Farsi asshole!" emmanated from the **FOG**. Immediately following the words, the boat rocked and a sickening sounding "Whump!" reverberated past Davecki's face. The whump reminded Davecki of the sound of Carl Anderson's face stopping a speeding softball during 6th grade recess. The next sound was harder. It was a heavy "Thunk" that caused Davecki's feet to vibrate. Then there was a wholesale crash that shook the boat and Davecki knew a body had fallen. Then there was a "rumble-thwack, rumble-thwack," and something bumped into Davecki's boot toe. He looked down. The **FOG** must be turning into fog, Davecki thought because he could see his toes. There, like a cat at his feet, a twelve pound downrigger bomb rocked. He bent over and picked up the lead ball.

"Ugh!" he involuntarily said as he lifted the heavy lead ball that had just rolled across the deck. It was covered with blood.

Now, this could mean two things, Davecki thought. It could be Chuckson's blood. It could be raghead blood. If it was raghead blood, which Davecki assumed it to be, it meant Chuckson had struck a blow against the enemy. Now, if this downrigger bomb had hit a man —er, person, Davecki politically corrected himself— anywhere other than the head, it would not have likely drawn blood. Unless of course the person was a hemophiliac with thin skin and no clothing to protect that flimsy skin. So, Davecki —who had always possessed a keen grasp of the obvious— concluded there had to be one hurting raghead nearby.

And, he thought, speaking of nearby, he was sure he was regaining a sense of place, for it seemed he could see a bit more of the transom on which he sat.

He looked left. Fog. But lighter looking fog. He looked right. Fog. But fog that was somewhat penetrable. He looked down. Low and behold he could see the box of the Bayliner's engine cover and, to his surprised eyes, he could see red. He rubbed his eyes realizing he was straining them. But it was a true, a bright red stream of blood was flowing out of the gloom, running across the deck, past his boot toes and out the wash hole in the corner.

Now, let's assume, Davecki counseled himself, that Captain John Chuckson was a true marine stalwart, believing in the old adage, "the Captain goes down with the ship." That would mean the other good guy in this seriously whacked scenario was aboard the Formula and not the IBM. So, unless a geyser of blood was squirting from Chuckson's wound and hosing down the IBM from afar, the blood at his feet had to be from the enemy.

So let's see, Davecki thought. There's someone in the water and there's someone bleeding on board. How many ragheads does a fishing trip make? Davecki wondered. If there were two he felt safe. If three or more his work wasn't done. So, he did what most good cops do when faced with superior confusion and questionable odds. He obeyed one of the first rules of law enforcement. He heeded the command, "Don't just do something, sit there!"

As he pondered the nature of his "sit-shee-ation," Davecki continued to observe that his environment was changing. It was getting lighter. He could hear better and noted that splashing sounds rose from the water behind and below him. That would be raghead number one, Davecki knew. Then another sound waltzed up to this ears. "Formula, Formula, this is the Coast Guard. Formula, do you read me?"

It was Chuckson's radio.

"Dave will you get that please? I'm a little busy right now," Chuckson's voice responded.

To Davecki's surprise, the captain's voice came from his right. The radio's voice came from his left.

"Ak-Beth moola coola mocha boat-cha," a voice came up from the water behind him. Davecki hoped the swimmer had also lost his weapon.

The cop was getting tired of keeping quiet. But he had to. What if there were more ragheads who wanted to hurt him?

"Dave?" Chuckson's voice came through the gloom again.

Davecki turned toward the sound to discover that the gloom wasn't gloom anymore. It was just veil type fog he could actually see through. What he saw was John Chuckson, Captain of the Formula, sitting on the mid-section of a middle-eastern type of guy who was bleeding profusely from a gash in his forehead. "Hey! This guy's only got one ear!" Chuckson yelled.

"Formula. Formula. This is the Coast Guard. Do you read me?"

"They're going to be pissed if you don't answer that, Dave," Chuckson said. The Captain grinned and nodded his chin toward Davecki who followed the fisherman's gaze. Davecki turned and looked over his left shoulder, and there, waiting patiently and looming out of the fog was the sleek hull of the Bertram. It was only a few feet away. A spry middle aged man or a moderately lethargic teenager could jump the gap between the two vessels easily. Which is what Davecki did. He keyed the mic and said, "Coast Guard, this is Formula. We've got a little problem here."

"Go ahead, Formula...."

"Yeah Coast Guard. This is Detective Alphonse Davecki of the Superior Police and I'm aboard the Formula. We've had a minor collision with a boat called IBM and have been shot at. The situation is under control, but there's heavy fog. Could you send a patrol?"

"Formula, this is the Coast Guard Station at Park Point. Fog? Did you say heavy fog?"

"Roger Coast Guard. We're about three miles up the north shore off Lester River or just beyond and we're in heavy fog. With one man —er, person— overboard, one man shot and one wounded in the head."

"Roger Formula. Copy that. Patrol boat scrambling as we speak. Say again... heavy fog? It's sunny and mild here with visibility unlimited.

Davecki looked around him. Though the myst was turning to mere mist, it still looked like fog. It felt like fog. It smelt like fog. He concluded, if fog could shit, this would shit so it must be fog. He keyed the mic and said, "It looks like fog to me Coast Guard."

"Roger that Formula. Hold your position. Help is on the way. We were calling to locate you, Detective. Your Chief of Police wants you to call him. Over."

"Roger that Coast Guard. The fog seems to be lifting. Will stand-by. Will call home." Davecki hooked the mic back into its holder and left the cabin. He emerged to visability that was rapidly improving. He could see both boats. He could see a man with a brown face and black hair treading water looking petrified. The man was looking directly at Davecki. "American pigdog," the man said.

"Nice to meet you too," Davecki said wishing he had his Glock.

The man started swimming for the IBM's diving platform. "Hold it," Davecki said.

The man kept swimming.

"Got a bogie coming aboard at six o'clock, John," Davecki yelled. He could see Chuckson was tying the hands of raghead number two with a rope.

"Got it," Chuckson answered. "Toss me the fish whacker will ya?"

Davecki reached into the Formula's gunwale pocket and extracted the foot and a half long hickory club stored there. It looked like a mini-baseball bat. In Chuckson's expert hand, the bat had conked many a flopping fish to death. He stood up and noted that the shoreline, a mile away, was now somewhat discernable. He turned in time to see Chuckson climb on to the diving platform of the ship next door. Chuckson reached out with his big Nike-clad foot and plunked the swarthy swimmer under the water with a sure kick to the top of the black haired head.

The swimmer sank and came up sputtering. Davecki loved Chuckson at that moment. The Captain was so elemental.

"Toss it," Chuckson said.

Davecki flipped the club through the air. Chuckson caught it and bent over. Years and years of experience hauling thousands and hundreds of flopping fish from the water showed as Chuckson reached out to the struggling sputtering Hadji in the water.

The man flailed at and tried to grab Chuckson's arms. Chuckson slapped the grasps away, grabbed a fist full of hair and yanked. Hadji yelped and before he could make another grab for Chuckson, the Captain whacked the hell out of him alongside the head with the fish whacker.

"That's for Yosemite," Chuckson said. He flipped the club back to Davecki who caught it as Chuckson reefed the unconscious man from the water to the platform. The IBM was low in the stern from the weight.

"Formula, Formula. This is the Handyman's Hooker. What the hell's going on over there?" the radio crackled.

Chuckson laughed. "That's Dr. Fish," he said grunting as his big frame hauled the body aboard. "Tell him we caught a couple of blood suckers!"

Davecki was about to go for the radio when a splash distracted him from watching Chuckson drag his catch onto the Bayliner's aft deck. He turned to see, surfacing at the back of the Formula, a scuba diver. The dry-suited diver was taking his/her mask off in the water. Davecki saw that he held something in his hand. "Throw your weapon aboard!" Davecki said using his command voice. The diver was startled and, after de-masking completely, tossed something to the deck. Davecki dipped down quickly to grab the item at his feet. As he held it up he couldn't help but be shocked. Why was he holding a geiger counter?

"I give up!" a man's voice said. His accent was Jordanian. Or, maybe it was Iranian? Who knew? It was Middle Eastern. "We are Iraqi diplomats! Do not harm us!" That answers that, Davecki thought.

"Come aboard slowly," Davecki said.

"Formula, Formula, this is Handyman's Hooker. Do you read me? What the hell's with this fog? Do you read me Formula? Do you require assistance?"

Davecki wanted to answer the call but he couldn't take his eye off the diver climbing out of the water. Luckily a scuba diver, Lloyd Bridges excepted (God rest his soul), fully equipped isn't much of a threat out of water. Davecki did the first thing that came to mind. He grabbed the landing net and jammed it down over the head, shoulders and tank of the diver.

"Stand up," Davecki commanded.

The diver struggled to his flippered feet. Davecki hauled forth and back on the net's handle as the diver rose. The motion made the net go further down on the diver's body, pinning the arms.

"Climb over. Sit!" Davecki said.

The diver complied silently.

"Formula, Formula, this is the Coast Guard. We're waiting for the bridge to clear and will be under way. Your position ETA fifteen minutes."

"Formula, Formula, this is Handyman's Hooker. Our lines are being cut. Will be alongside in three," Dr. Fish added to the radio chatter.

"Stay!" Davecki yelled at the diver. He reached into the gunwale well again and pulled out a stringer. He tied the hands and feet of the diver and went to the radio. He was about to key the mic when he remembered.

Davecki put the mic back. He dashed over to the rod holder on the port side, pulled out the rod and started twisting on the Garcia's crank. After a couple of dozen rapid reels, Davecki could feel the tug of the giant salmon. "He's still hooked!" Davecki shouted.

"Handyman's Hooker, Handyman's Hooker, this is Captain John Chuckson aboard the IBM," Davecki heard behind him.

"Go ahead," the radio crackled.

"Hey Doc. Hurry it up will yah? Dave's got a twenty plus pound salmon on and we need your landing net pronto!" Chuckson's alarmed voice trilled through the air.

"Hot damn! Be there in two!" the radio answered."

Davecki resumed his battle with the fish, as the distant roar of the Handyman's Twin 454 big block Chevy engines resounded across the water.

Nobody wanted to lose a trophy fish like the one still on the end of Davecki's line.

16

"**W**ell, what was I supposed to do, Chief?"
Davecki asked. He was sitting in Chief Callahan's
office. Why are police chiefs always Irish? Davecki
wondered. It was no mystery why Richard "Big Dick"
Callahan was Chief of Police in Superior. His Mom
and Dad and Grandpa were cops. B.D. had what it
took to rise through the ranks and stay at the top.

He was attentive to detail. His office was neat.
His desk organized. His grooming habits were precise. His gray hair was combed to perfection. His
salt and pepper beard was trimmed smartly. Callahan
was stocky. He had been the toughest kid in his army
unit and brought the street smarts he'd learned while
growing up in Kenosha, Wisconsin to the Army boxing ring. Inside the squared-circle, Callahan showed
his moxey. He was All Army and he pounded the hell
out of midshipman Corey "Ding Dong" Davis for a
shot at the Olympic boxing team. Too bad Vietnam
ruined his plans. But, it was for the best, because
Callahan met Army nurse Dode Bergquist in 'Nam.
"Good morning Vietnam," were the first words
Callahan heard Dode speak after he came out of se-
dation during his stay at the M.A.S.H. unit. Everyone
in Callahan's squad was required to visit the M.A.S.H.
Something about humping through the jungle on night
patrol made it mandatory to get ambushed and shot.
Dode brought Callahan home to Superior.

The rest was, and is, history because Chief
Callahan wrote a book called, *Stop It or I'll Shoot in*

the Name of the Law, which became a local bestseller and turned the Chief into a minor celebrity known and loved by all. There was even talk of a mayoral bid. But that was not Davecki's concern. The detective looked at the pair of Golden Glove mitts hanging from the wall and he finished his sentence, "Let them shoot seventeen holes in us?"

"You were out of your jurisdiction. You were supposed to call for the Duluth P.D. and the Coast Guard," Callahan said.

"Sure B.D., I would have but there was this little problem. We were being shot at."

The Chief toyed with his coffee cup. It said Chesapeake on the side. As the Chief spun the cup in his capable hands, Davecki saw a bagel screenprinted on the opposite side of the mug. "Why was that Dave? Was it not that you were in fact ramming them for no good reason other than to provoke them?"

"You sound like that blankety-blank blonde D.A., Connie O'Konek," Davecki said shifting in his chair.

"I have been talking to the comely Connie. In fact, all I'm doing here is helping you make a case for the D.A. when it comes trial time," Callahan said.

Davecki sighed. He knew Callahan was just doing his job, just doing him a favor by dressing him down and pressuring him the way a good defense lawyer would. "I told you B.D., it was an accident. We were landing Big Bertha and we weren't paying attention to the helm.

"This is common practice? Letting a boat wander all around Lake Superior without a driver is normal?"

Something in the Water

Davecki folded his hands. He envisioned sunrise over Lake Superior. His breathing deepened. He wasn't to the Our Father stage, but Callahan's questioning might get him there. "Yes, it's common Chief. Hell, we were only going a mile an hour. Anyone with half a brain would see, hear and practically smell another boat coming and yell out," Davecki explained.

"And you can produce this Big Bertha?"

"She's at the taxidermy shop now. She'll be ready in plenty of time, way before any trial," Davecki said.

Callahan didn't respond. He took a sip of coffee and looked out the window of his corner office. He didn't deserve the nickname P.D., even if he was a pencil pusher, Davecki thought. If the rookies who called him that knew he was on them all the time only for their own good, they'd call him B.D. or Chief or something kinder.

"So what are we going to do about Gronsby's murder?"

Davecki reconfigured himself in the chair. "I still think they did it Chief."

"Well that thinking is stinking, Detective. We need proof, evidence!"

"I know that sir. But they shot at Chuckson and me. They were searching for weapons grade plutonium in the barrels. Gronsby wanted the barrels removed, got too curious about why the IBM was always over the dumping sights and they killed him."

"Dave," Callahan said as he stood up and walked over to the four drawer file in the corner. He hung one elbow over the cabinet and spun the cup in his hands. "You're grasping. I believe Akmed's confession. Why would an Iraqi terrorist want to kill Gronsby? He said they didn't murder anyone."

"Beg your pardon Chief, but they were planning to blow up New York City with a homemade nuclear bomb."

"Well, of course they were. Why wouldn't they? It makes perfect sense that they just wanted closure on the World Trade Center thing. Why, anyone would feel bad about such a miserable failure. Any terrorist worth his or her salt would never jeopardize the mission too early. Killing Gronsby would have put the greater good at risk, "Callahan said.

"So what can we get 'em on?" Davecki asked.

"Connie says Faisal and Saisel will go away for a long time. Assault with a deadly weapon, illegal entry, they'll cool their heels at Waupon," Callahan said.

"What about Akmed?"

"Diplomatic immunity holds. He'll be heading home in a week or so. Saisel and his brother will do time though."

Davecki listened to Callahan's last comment and thought about all the time Thurber Gronsby had spent on the barrel raising project. He mapped the dump sites. He made a hundred trips out to the sites. He observed boat traffic and he interviewed anyone on the water who would talk to him. He chummed bloody meat to the media sharks as best he could and he never ever let the subject rest. And for all his efforts, there was never, not once, any serious interest in lifting those barrels off the lake's floor. Until now. Now, thanks to

Akmed and his cousins, the whole world was clamoring to retrieve the barrels.

"Who'd a thunk it, hey Dave?" Callahan said.

"Huh?"

Callahan smiled and walked toward his desk. He showed how much cops think alike when he said, "Who'd a thunk Thurber Gronsby couldn't get barrel one off the bottom but a couple of terrorists and a diplomat from halfway around the world could get the whole kit and kaboodle coming up in record time."

"Kit and kaboodle?"

"Up yours, Davecki. You know what really gets me though?" the Chief said sitting down.

"No I don't," Davecki said.

"What gets me is the amount of money they spent. It must have cost millions to buy that freighter, put in the false bottom, register it, crew it, sail it up the seaway..."

"To say nothing of the cost of that mini-sub," Davecki interrupted.

Callahan scowled at his detective. "Why didn't they just buy a nuke from Russia?"

"Like I said," Davecki answered, "I think they just wanted a sunny vacation in balmy Superior."

"Up yours Davecki. Now get out there and find out who killed Thurber Gronsby."

17

Davecki kept the Mustang in third. The speed limit on London Road was thirty miles-an-hour. Everyone did forty, some fifty, but not Davecki. No. He had to go thirty. Not to piss off the long line of cars, pickups and Monson semis piled up behind him, but because the Duluth cops often worked speed on London Road. He couldn't give 'em the satisfaction of pinching a Superior cop.

The Mustang galloped past Brighton Beach. The usual crowd of onlookers were present. Some had expensive spotting scopes set up on tripods to see the action better. Davecki kept driving. He briefly considered taking the freeway up to McQuade Road and turning down, but opted for the scenic highway, or as it was now called, Bob Dylan Drive.

As the cop rolled northeast up the shore, he saw the curious and intrigued sitting in lawn chairs. Some were cooking on hibachis, others were taking photographs with long lenses. It was a regular spectacle. Travelers from around the country came to watch the barrels come up. Most of the observers were from the Twin Cities. They were concerned about "their" lake. After all, the only reason Duluth-Superior existed was to provide a convenient playground for the city sucker scum of the Twin Cities. If the powers that be had known the economic boon raising the barrels was going to be, they'd have listened to Gronsby years ago.

Davecki felt sad as he drove. He was so sure the Iraqis had killed Gronsby. But until Orion Niroma,

Something in the Water

from the Madison Crime Lab, told him that Gronsby had drowned, that there was not one scintilla of evidence on Gronsby's corpse to connect the terrorists, Davecki held on to some hope that the case was solved. Unfortunately, Niroma was the world's foremost expert on DNA testing, forensic evidence and, apparently, scintillas. Why a scientist of Niroma's stature would want to raise what amounted to fur bearing rats was beyond him. To each his own, Davecki thought as he motored the Mustang into the parking lot of the Lakevilla Castille. He liked to stop at the Faux Chauteau though he didn't like driving through the speed zone on highway Sixty-One. The corrupt constable there, besides selling confiscated beer to minors, was always eager to collect a little lunch money for the Governor by over estimating the speed of cars with out of state plates. Davecki would get tea and a bagel, sit by the window and watch the going's on aboard the barges off shore. In the intervening weeks since the Iraqi incident over 500 of the two thousand six hundred odd barrels had been raised. Only three of them were found to contain the radioactive material the terrorists sought. According to Akmed, his sister had indicated there were ten or so barrels of material that came from Goodyear Atomic in Chillicothe, Ohio. With the one confiscated from the false-bottomed bulk freighter, there were only six more to be found.

Davecki climbed the rocky staircase and, at the stoney stairhead, resisted the urge to do a Rocky dance. He didn't feel exhilarated. He felt depressed. Inside the cafe, Lexie the waitress from Calgary greeted him like the old customer he had become. Usually the sight of Lexie cheered him for, like the bride of Frankenstein, she owned huge tracts of land. As he sat at the corner table and said yes to Roxanne's question of, "The usual?" his dismay slid toward suicidal ideation as he spotted Robby Rosenstern coming up the stairs.

"Damn," he said.

Lexie looked out the window following Davecki's expletive and said, "He's been waiting all morning."

Robby was a good kid. The only problem was, he worked as a reporter for the Snooze Tribune. The cub reporter walked up and smiled. "Can I buy your tea this morning, Detective?"

"That's a violation of your code of ethics, son. To say nothing of offering a kindness to one of 'The Unwashed Masses' from Superior," Davecki said.

"I'm not working," the reporter said and sat down.

Lexie brought two bagels, two tea pots, a dish of lemon slices and a decanter of honey, all in her two dainty hands. She was a real pro. "Here you go boys. Try not to break any furniture," she said and left.

The first time Rosenstern had approached Davecki here, they'd argued loudly and Davecki stomped out knocking a chair over on his way. In retrospect, the argument was good because Davecki had returned to the jail mad enough to get Faisal to talk. The three Iraqis seemed quite content to sit silently for years of questioning. Davecki figured they were waiting to be beaten and tortured before talking. So, when Robby triggered his rage, he returned to the jail, picked Faisal, the terrorist with one ear, and broke a chair over the table.

He talked. Then Akmed caved in after being assured by O'Konek that the diplomatic immunity trick would work.

So he owed Kenny. This meeting was payback.

"So?" Rosenstern said.

"Sew buttons on your underwear," Davecki said. And, the joke that his mother used to make actually improved his mood. His gloom was lifting and he was looking forward to talking to Robby, answering all the questions he could about the case. He thought of what his therapist Toby Christianson often said, "The opposite of depression is expression."

"Underwear aside, Davecki, what'sup?"

"Well, Akmed's going home. Saisel and Faisal are going to prison."

"Did they kill Thurber Gronsby?"

"I still think they did, but there's no evidence."

"So how did they come to Lake Superior in search of atomic bomb material?"

"Nuclear bomb material, you should know the difference, Kenny."

"I didn't grow up hiding under my school desk during air raid drills. I'm not fixated on the instantaneous destruction of the world as we know it."

Davecki studied the kid, "You need to get out more son," he said.

Rosenstern looked out the window, eyed the circus across the road, across the water.

He's thinking about my comment Davecki

thought. He said, "You can't take the world so seriously son."

Rosenstern blinked and said, "Point taken. So, Why? Who? What? Where? When?"

Davecki added, "And sometimes how?" as he pulled his teabag from the pot. He slung the sotted sack of English Teatime into the spoon's bowl and garotted the swollen leaves to secrete the remaining beverage into the stainless steel teapot.

"Come on officer."

"Detective," Davecki said as he squeezed a lemon slice above his cup. He tore the honey packet open and squirted the amber fluid into the bottom of the black mug. "I hate black cups. Can't see if they're clean," he commented. He poured tea and said, "I'll have to train Lexie to put water in both the pot and the cup," he said while stirring silently. "You know it's bad luck to clunk your cup when stirring?" he asked with a grin.

Rosenstern sighed and looked out the window again. It was torture, Davecki thought, to keep the exclusive from the kid any longer. He sipped his drink. "Perfect," he said.

"Great." Rosenstern said without taking his eyes off the lake and Davecki knew he had to relent. "Akmed's sister married Samuel Jackson Solongstrum, a union trucker from Minneapolis. The guy was hauling barrels from Honeywell to Duluth during the dumping operation. Seems there were some contraband barrels that got added into the loads. Seems there was a lot of cash moving around to keep everyone silent. Seems these stray barrels were from Goodyear Atomic in Ohio and were vanishing into Lake Superior's depths to be forgotten ever more."

"What changed that?"

Davecki liked the kid's questions. They were simple. He sipped more tea. He was definitely feeling better. "Thirty years later Akmed visited his sister. You know how it is with those Iraqis."

"No I don't," Robby said finally attending to his tea service. He added, "Gotta steep four minutes."

Davecki explained, "There are no secrets in Muslim families. Talk got around to the unfinished business at the World Trade Center and sis says bro should nuke it."

"Bro says there's no way he can sneak a nuclear device across the border. Sis says why not build one with material already in the country. Bro says that'd be just peachy if all the plutonium wasn't in the middle of a bank in somebody else's name."

"Very funny," Robby said bringing his tea cup to lips virtually obscured by his huge beard.

"So Sis tells Akmed that her hubby helped haul plutonium to Duluth.

"How'd she know that?" Rosenstern asked.

"You ever hear of pillow talk? Or were you born too late for that too?"

"Very very funny officer."

"Detective."

They sat in silence for a bit. They looked out at the lake. Their gaze sailed above the heads of the observers across the highway to the barge operation beyond. After several moments of silence, Robby said, "So it can't feel very good to have the Gronsby thing unsolved. Who do you think did that if it wasn't the ragheads?"

"Such language from a liberal. I'm shocked, Robby."

"Live with it."

"How do you know the terrorists didn't kill Gronsby?"

"Because," the reporter smiled, "The official charges were filed late yesterday and I read them early this morning. There's nothing about murder in the complaint."

"Very impressive."

"So?"

"So what?" Davecki parroted.

"So who killed Gronsby?"

Davecki had only one little inkling and he was not about to share his hunch with Rosenstern.

"Go figure, Robby. You're the bright rising reporter."

"That's your job, Detective."

"Thank you Reporter."

They smiled at each other and raised their cups. Davecki was saying, "Ahhh," just as his phone chirped inside his bomber's pocket.

"Yeah," Davecki said into the device at his head. "Yeah? Really? Okay. I'll be right down."

He punched a key and stood while pocketing the phone. "What'sup?" Robby asked.

"Off the record?"

Something in the Water

"Sure."

"Say it."

"Okay! Really, really off the record," Rosenstern said.

"They opened a barrel at the decontamination site at the Port Authority."

"And?" Robby said, his eyebrows raising.

"They found a body inside."

"Wait!" We haven't talked about your mysterious fog yet."

"Gotta go, Robby. Maybe Captain Chuckson can help you there. The sea is his specialty."

"He's on vacation to Isle Royal! Davecki!" Robby yelled.

"Talk to Callahan," Davecki yelled back as he rushed out of the room. He didn't knock any furniture over this time.

He was definitely happy now. Something else was in the water and he had been able to do some serious dirt to Callahan by sending Robby as a gift. Maybe it wasn't such a bad day after all. He jumped in the Stang and turned away from his original destination. After tea he had intended to go further up the shore to Stoney Point. The rocky beach was one of his favorite places. But now there was something even more appealing than a good sit-and-think next to Mother Superior. The Big Lake had coughed up another body and spit it out like a foul goober. Maybe there were some answers lying on the floor of the Decom Center at the Port Authority.

18

Davecki took the freeway back to Duluth. Humming along the four lane, feeling happy to have avoided Rosenstern's question about the fog, Davecki decided to take some of the excitement he felt about the body in the barrel and apply it to that particular climatalogical mystery.

The Mustang sped along between the encroaching trees. To look at the facts, Davecki thought, right here, right now, this moment, there was no evidence that there was even a teeny-weeny lake nearby, let alone the Mother of All Lakes. All he could see was road, sky and forest.

Davecki shivered. The trouble was, if you could call it trouble he thought, the lake was there. It occupied a huge spot in the geography and a huge spot in his psyche.

He'd grown up swimming in it. He'd fished it, pissed in it, made love in it, walked on it, flew over it, drove around it, smelled it from afar, dreamt of it, drank it, boiled it, threw it at his friends, threw his friends in it, looked at it for hours at a stretch. He'd seen it practically every day of his life. He'd missed it when traveling. The lake called to him from afar, spoke to him with its waves. The speech was sometimes quiet; little lapping waves that felt like kitten kisses on his toes. Then there was the shouting. It was usually November. But not always. In Cornucopia, the waves would crash along the Corp of

Something in the Water

Engineer's Pier shooting a moving geyser fifty feet in the air for two hundred yards. When he was fifteen, looking at Old Faithful for the first time, Davecki thought of the spectacular sprays of Lake Superior storms and wondered why people were so het up over that Wyoming squirt.

Then there were the magnificent brawls of storm that crashed into the western end of the lake. Some of them made Corny's storms seem mere tempests in a teapot. Those nor'easters literally pounded the shoreline and made anyone watching understand their own frailty.

Davecki looked about him. "Where are you?" he said out loud. And from within he knew the answer. He felt a huge part of him answer. "Here." He felt as if a full two thirds of his spiritual topography had just said "Right here inside you."

He was suddenly uncomfortable. He wanted to avoid the thought he'd already had. He thought about sleeping on her beaches. He thought about bonfires and UFO watching. He recalled canoe trips along shores both rocky and wooded. Boat rides to the caves, cold sand on his hot balls while making love. But he was doomed. The thought just waited. Waited until he was done distracting himself.

"For a cop you're too damn cerebral," he said out loud. He pounded a four count out on the steering wheel with the heels of his palm. Robert Palmer. Rosey Palm. He thought of whipping it out. The last time he did that was decades ago.

And then the thought got impatient. It got up in

his throat and forced itself up into his consciousness. "The lake is alive."

Davecki turned on the radio, "Now I'm a believer, Yeah, yeah, yeah, I couldn't leave her if I tried," blared out of 109.2 FM.

"Damn," he said and shut the radio off fast. So what you're saying Davecki, Davecki said to himself, is that Lake Superior herself is manipulating events to get herself cleaned up? His mind reeled. There were too many conversations going on inside him. A headache appeared just above his cheekbones. He knew it would be behind his eyes soon and that shortly thereafter it would possess his entire brain like a nor'eastern possessed Lake Superior, like Lake Superior possessed his soul.

"Wham," he whacked the steering wheel. The dash rattled. Thought myself into another migraine, he said to himself. He reached over and opened the glove-box even though he already knew there was no aspirin there. He always had plans to keep a bottle of pain killers in the car but it never happened.

He felt for the new Glock under his arm. Ten m.m. A real pain killer. He imagined the coolness of the barrel resting in the socket of his left eye. Some migraines were like that.

"You need a vacation, Dave," he said out loud. He shut his mouth hard. Just clamped it shut like a dog catching a fly. He hated himself when his brain went wild like this. But then, he loved this hyper-aware state too, because, from it he often was able to reach a solid conclusion. It usually took a while to sift through the mental chaff, but there was always some good to be gleaned from the "insanity chatter" as he called it.

Usually a good result took time. But not this day. This day was different. Davecki saw the familiar rise to the end of the freeway. He saw the big yellow signs announcing the demise of four lanes. He tugged the steering wheel left, unaware that he was about to change forever. He was conscious of his headache. The mental/spiritual work he'd been doing had retrenched as a simple headache when he crested the rising turn to the left and saw the big sea shining waters.

The lake was glowing. It shone in the sun. It was happy. He recalled Brooks Robertson's prognostication that the lake would glow. When the plutonium angle came out he'd thought the old clairvoyant had meant "glow" in the nuclear waste sense. But as the vision of the lake engulfed him he realized Robertson too had concluded that the lake was alive. He realized that, for forty some years, he too, Dave Davecki, cop, cynic, scientist wannabe, demander of proof, expecter of evidence, had always acceded to the prescience of Lake Superior.

He descended the hill, approached London Road, and hardly saw the gathered masses as they hovered around to commemorate the cleansing of the Mother of all Lakes. A huge wave of relief surged through him like a big sweeping roller that didn't crest and break into froth. The belief effort drowned his denial and he openly admitted to himself what he knew to be true. The lake called to him while he was at Lost Creek Home, lured him to go fishing, made the fog specifically to help, specifically to get those barrels expunged from her bosom. He looked left at the barges with their crews working at raising the barrels and knew the cancer was being removed.

He smiled. There was something in that water. It had saved his life. Now, as he shifted down for the slow cruise along London Road, he felt it was time to return the favors of a lifetime. He was going to figure out who killed Thurber Gronsby, the man responsible for saving Lake Superior.

19

Davecki idled past the protesters. Well, they weren't protesters. They were celebrators. The Port Authority had set up a gate and a guard house to keep the pushy ones off the property and allow only authorized personnel in. But the pro... no, celebrators had set up a side show camp between UPS and the entrance in hopes of attracting some media attention. There were tents, chairs, and a campfire consuming precious resources. Several expensive sport utility vehicles that were utterly unresponsible for the consumption of finite fossil fuels crouched nearby. There was a beat-up old Suburban with the back doors open wide and a sign advertising little plastic barrels for sale at two for five bucks. A celebrator grinned into Davecki's car from the other side and waved a sign that said, "Thurber lives."

"I wish," Davecki said.

Another sign held by a short woman with a big smile said, "Barrels of (NOT) fun." Davecki had seen the lady at the Barnes and Noble store on Central Entrace many times. She was one of the goddesses of the place.

Another sign held by a scruffy man in a green fatigue jacket and camouflage pants said, "Roll out the barrels, we'll have a barrel of scum." Davecki wondered if the fellow was a Vet or a wanna-be warrior who couldn't stomach the thought of actually killing a real enemy but found no remorse in his soul over the killing of an industry or a way of life.

At the guard shack a mouse-haired man peered down from the window into Davecki's angular face. Davecki flashed his badge at the guard. "Hey Tom," the cop said. The guard replied, "Detective Davecki. When this is all over, if you want, you can borrow my motor home for a vacation."

"I need it now Thomas," Davecki said.

The guard looked astonished. His handlebar mustache rose a full inch.

"Just kidding, Tom," Davecki said and he let the clutch out. He drove right, taking the road past Lafarge Cement and headed toward the east warehouse.

Davecki felt a shudder twiddle up his spine as he realized the ground he was treading on was sacred. The Chippewa had tried to buy it from the Port Authority. With their tremendous wealth harvested from the nest eggs of millions of senior citizens, the band had first tried to buy all of Rice's Point. Then they went for the one hundred acres of Port land claiming that their legendary ancestor Three Eagles was buried here.

Davecki didn't know what to think of that claim. He'd read in the Superior Library that Indians tended to bury their dead wherever they breathed their last. So he figured it was probable, but, he thought, impossible to prove.

What the Chippewa settled for was to have one of their own appointed as Port Director. The venerable former director retired to become the Superintendant of the U.S.S. DeMoines State Veterans Park in "Coupla Harbors." Mavis Strongbird took over as Captain of the Port Authority ship. Davecki drove past the tall sculpture of Three Eagles and nodded. He had the urge to do the sign of the cross. Didn't. He crossed the railroad tracks and got off the sandy road onto the concrete. Ahead of him were an assortment of barges, tugs, and cranes with skeletal arms extending into the pale blue sky. Forklifts scurried about like beetles. Longshoremen leaned on whatever was handy.

As he drove he remembered how, in college at UW-Superior, he and his friends would grab their hockey sticks and go on "rat smacks." They'd drive onto Port Authority property after midnight and park. Then everyone but one girl would get out and sit on the hood in the darkness armed with hockey sticks. After twenty minutes of silence, the girl in the car would turn on the car's headlights illuminating hundreds of rats that had returned to feeding on the spilled grain. Everyone would bail off the hood and smack as many rats as they could. It was a crazy three minutes that ended in much huffing and puffing. Then they'd move further down the warf and do it again.

Another favorite thing Davecki and his friends did as college students was to sneak aboard moth-balled lakers like the William Irvin and sing hymns in the holds. The acoustics were unearthly. The effect on the soul profound.

Davecki shook off the memories and parked next to a green Jaguar XJ-12 and walked over to a shoddy looking kid with long hair. "'Sup?" Davecki said trying to sound like he was twenty-something.

The kid looked at the cop and frowned. "Found

some stiff. Can't work. They'll lay us off for the day is my guess," the kid said.

"You Shinob?" Davecki said wanting to show some familiarity with Anishaanabe vernacular.

"Yeah, the kid said.

"What happened?"

The kid looked at him and said, "You're the cop."

Davecki wondered if it was that obvious or if he had had a run-in with the kid in the past. As he wondered, they both looked toward Davecki's Mustang where another car had just parked. It was an old cobalt blue Volvo. Robby Rosenstern got out. He was talking on a cell phone. He waved and headed toward the warehouse.

"Guess I better get going," Davecki said. He started for the warehouse when the kid's voice turned him.

"Hey Davecki!"

"Yeah?" Davecki said, figuring the kid must be remembering him from a court appearance or something.

"Thanks for helping this get going."

"No problem," Davecki said and turned away.

"Hey Davecki!"

Davecki turned again, "What?"

"Never say Shinob to a Shinob. It's not cool," the kid grinned.

"Right," he said and planned to take that advice as he turned away.

"Davecki."

The cop turned again to see that the First American or whatever he was, had left his lean-to and was jogging over to him, "Can I come?"

Davecki had no idea if he could or not. But it didn't matter to him. He was unsure about his ability to get in himself, after all, it was Minnesota, the land where everything is done differently.

The two men walked into the cavernous warehouse. Huge piles of banded waste paper bales which were destined for recycling at Superior Recycled Fiber Industries towered on either side of the door. Ahead, down the foreboding corridor made by the massive stacks of paper, a wad of people stood around a squad car with its Jetsonics flashing. As they walked the kid said, "You know how Indians name their kids?"

"Nope," Davecki said.

The kid rubbed his hands together. "Well, it's like this. One day a little Indian kid asked his dad, 'Dad, how do Indians come up with all these cool names?' The dad smiled, looked wise and said, 'Well, after the baby is born the father goes outside and looks around. If he sees three eagles he names the baby that.' Then the father looked down at the boy and said, 'Why do you ask, Two Dogs Fucking?'" The jokester laughed loudly.

Davecki didn't know if he should laugh or not. It might be uncool which is what Indians seemed to want all whites to be. But it was clear he should have when the kid stopped laughing and looked at him.

So Davecki let his laugh out and then they both chuckled. They walked from between the paper bales into a section of the warehouse where giant sacks of talc used in the papermaking process were stored. The piles weren't as high as the paper. On the lake side of the building a rail car was visible through the open doors of the warehouse. Two people stood next to a silent forklift. One was a man. The woman was smoking a cigarette.

"I don't like women who smoke," Davecki said.

"Me neither," the kid said and added, "that's my sister."

Davecki figured he couldn't say anything right to this kid. He decided to shut up around Indians. They approached a group of people standing next to a wooden traffic barricade. A heated discussion was going on. Davecki nodded toward Rosenstern. The reporter nodded back.

An older Indian man with long braids was saying a lot. Davecki picked it up on, "Could be sacred."

A tall woman answered, "Come on Jim. In a barrel? Give it up. Let the cops handle it." The speaker was Mavis Strongbird. The tall woman looked at Davecki and his chum. "And who have you dragged home now, Jimmy?"

"Aw Ma," the long-haired kid said. He shuffled his feet. "This is Dave Davecki."

Strongbird's face brightened. "Thank you, Mr. Davecki, for getting all this started," she said and stuck out her hand.

Davecki was embarrassed. He grabbed the tall woman's hand and knew how she got the first part of her last name.

A uniformed cop behind Strongbird pointed at

Davecki. "He can't come in here. I got my orders." He pointed at Rosenstern, "And that guy too. He's out of here. No press. I got my orders," the cop repeated.

Strongbird let go of Davecki's hand and turned to the cop. "Now Jim..."

Davecki couldn't believe the number of Jim's present.

"....This is my turf and I can understand no press, but a fellow officer of the law from our sister city across the bay? It wouldn't look good in the papers if it came out that you were keeping our local hero from helping."

"Hey that's a great angle," Robby said.

Jim the cop looked worried.

"I'll take responsibility," Strongbird said.

Jim the cop looked relieved and said, "Okay."

Strongbird gestured to Davecki and started walking around the squad car.

Davecki followed. Jimmy followed Davecki.

"Not you," the cop said putting his hand in front of the Indian.

Strongbird intervened. "Don't be silly Jim. He's my son. Come along Jimmy."

The cop shrugged and let his arm drop. The entire Superior Senior High marching band could have walked past the barricade at that moment. As Davecki passed, Robby pointed at him and mouthed, "You." Then the reporter shaped an, "O". Then he pointed at his chest and mouthed, "Me."

Davecki grinned and nodded.

The entourage walked into the containment area. There were barrels everywhere. Water covered the floor. Forklifts, wash stations, radiation suits, tools, a two-ton Ford truck with a Barko loader mounted on back, several hand trucks, a couple of electric fork lifts and three people were present in the make-shift room within a room made from giant sheets of plastic draped and stapled over a quickly assembled wooden framework.

The group walked up and looked down at the object the three men stood around. Davecki saw something he didn't expect. The corpse wasn't all shot to hell like all of the long dead bodies he'd seen. This one looked like an Egyptian mummy. "Wow!" Davecki said.

"Don't look too bad for a dead guy," Jimmy said.

"Hush!" Mavis said. She glared at her son.

A man in a gray sport coat, maroon denim shirt and no tie said, "I'm Dr. Tim Groady, pathologist at the UMD School of Medicine."

All Jims and Tims for today then is it? Davecki thought.

"This is Detective Davecki," Strongbird said.

"Nice to meet ya," Tim said, "And thanks."

Davecki wished everyone would stop thanking him. He didn't do anything special. "What's the deal?" he said pointing his nose toward the loose assembly of flesh sprawled next to an old barrel. The corpse had hair to its shoulders. The face looked leathery.

"The deal is, at thirty seven degrees and lacking any significant oxygen, there was virtually no decay.

147

Something in the Water

At least no significant decomposition.

Davecki thought of the Beethoven decomposing joke and also noted the lack of stench. The body had an old style leather jacket on. Gray-brown hands stuck out of the jacket arms. But the arms were crooked.

Tim noticed Davecki studying the body's arms. "The legs too. Broken to fit it into the space I suspect," Dr. Tim said.

A second man in the first group spoke. "We're going to send it to the cities. To the crime lab." Davecki knew this guy. It was the Duluth Chief of Police, Larry "Cat" Stevens. The third well-dressed man Davecki thought he knew, but couldn't place.

"Any chance I could get my guy from Madison to get in on the exam?" Davecki asked.

"Who?" Stevens asked.

"Orion Niroma. He's that expert. The guy who positively identified JFK's brain when they found it in Bush's house."

"Oh, that guy. Yeah, he's good. Don't bother me none," Steven's said. "I'll let 'em know at the lab."

The silent third man stuck out his hand. He wore spiffy loafers. "I'm Nick Navarone, Detective, and thanks."

Davecki shook the man's hand. He was astounded.

"Any clue? Any idea, Detective?" Navarone said looking at the corpse.

Davecki had only two certainties. One he kept to himself. It was that he needed a vacation badly. The second he shared. "All I know for sure is, this guy didn't kill Thurber Gronsby," he said staring in disbelief at the Italian union man.

20

In lieu of Cancun, Davecki went to Superior Design and Coffees. No better coffee existed within one hundred and sixty-eight miles, plus, it was the best place in town to go cozy. Davecki first frequented the place during college when it was Dave's Cave. Dave Kaner was an old grocer who, after his wife died, took to living in his store. You could go there any time of the night or day and get a six-pack of Schlitz, stale Banana Flips or Ho Ho's so old they chewed like venison jerky. Then two punks beat Dave to death and Davecki visited the Cave a few last times during the investigation. Kaner's body was found behind a counter next to the wall on the left as you enter. For years, the spot in the Nottingham building was vacant. Then Nancy and Tom took a risk and opened a coffee shop.

Davecki, his penchant for nick names and continuity showing, dubbed the place Nancy's Nook in honor of Dave's Cave. He liked unwinding at Nancy's better than any of the numerous bars in town for several reasons. First, there was no smoke. He hated it when the no smoking section in a restaurant was infested with the billowing clouds of a thousand smouldering Camels.

The second reason Davecki liked Nancy's Nook was he could overhear conversations. And third, when having his own chat, he didn't have to strain his voice to talk. The fourth reason was Nancy wore jeans better than anyone in town. The fifth was Tom, with his movie star good looks and stellar smile, talked to Davecki like he was a normal human and not a cop.

The sixth reason he could never recall until after he left the place. But when he was well down the street he always noticed himself feeling much calmer. Davecki thought about this contradiction as he watched Karla the Comley Coffee Queen pump his Cinnimon Mild from the thermos on the back bar. Karla was from Sleepy Eye, Minnesota and she was cute. She also liked camping in the winter and drinking beer at the Anchor.

Davecki put four quarters and a dime down on the counter and dug in the penny cup to bring the total to one fifteen. He poured milk in while Karla initialed his coffee card. "In Canada they call coffee with milk *regular coffee*," Davecki said.

"Really?" a cheerful voice from the tiny kitchen behind the cooler called. It was Dave the delivery dude. Dave was the fastest caffeine pusher in Superior. His old truck didn't look like much, but he and the old beater could get a coffee fix to a desperate addict in record time if the need was great. "That's cool," Dave said coming around the cooler from the kitchen. Davecki's eyes bulged. He was completely bald.

"You shaved your head!"

"Yeah, neat huh?"

Stirring his *regular coffee*, Davecki knew the vice squad was lucky this crowd had chosen to sell the last legal drug.

Davecki took his yellow mug and walked toward

his favorite spot, the Quarter Moon Chair. As he tucked himself in for a good sit-and-think, he thought, If caffeine calms me down then I must be a coff-a-holic. Then, as he worked his way into a perfectly awesome slouch, he realized if someone addicted to alcohol was an alcoholic, then he had to be a caffein*ic*.

He'd dubbed the divan the Quarter Moon Chair for it's crescent shape of course, and also for a song sung by the Loons, a well known local folk trio. The lyrics went, "Sing me a Chippewa story under the quarter moon." The article of furniture looked uncomfortable. It was a discarded booth section from the old Chef's Restaurant on Tower Avenue. Few people sat in it. Even Davecki had to be forced into it during a serious moment of over-crowding one lunch time. He'd discovered, if he slouched outrageously, the booth was wonderfully comfy. Almost as nice as Cancun and way less costly.

A seventh reason Davecki liked Nancy's Nook was the fact that Nancy's family used to own the old Capitol Tea Rooms at Eleventh and Tower. When he was a lad, Davecki's mother and aunt brought him to the Tea Rooms during shopping expeditions in the big city. Leaving the hustle and bustle of Tower Avenue and walking into the stately atmosphere of the Tea Rooms seemed ultimately cosmopolitan to the amazed boy. The Tea Room was long and dark with a counter on the left that seemed to stretch to infinity. On the right was a row of booths with incredibly tall backs made of dark wood. It all seemed so elegant, so sophisticated to the youngster. Tucked into the corner of those tall-backed booths, listening to the adults talk, he felt worldly and confident, secure in the all too frantic city that was so unlike his sedate home town.

Davecki slouched himself into his nook within the Nook intending to forget about the barrel affair. He took a sip of coffee and did what he always did, kept on keeping on. He was as obsessive as anyone when it came to solving murders.

A picture of Nick Navarone popped into his mind's eye. The guy had to be eighty, but still, he looked pretty damn good. And he was still a force to be reckoned with. He was running a well oiled union machine. Longshoremen, teamsters, CIO, Boilermakers, Pipefitters, the whole spectrum of organizations that held the fabric of society together, or so Navarone's people claimed. And, Davecki thought, it was a claim that was true to some extent, afterall, when UPS shut down, the country sort of freaked out.

Davecki put his feet up on the chair and shook his head. He was here to escape the case not rehearse it. But, like a Rottweiler with a bone, he was unable to let go. Fortunately, there were other forces at work. The door opened and in walked a spiffy blond.

Yet another reason to like the Nook, Davecki said to himself as he watched the woman close the door. She walked past and ignored him. Davecki smiled. She had thirteen places to sit where it would be impossible to chat. That was another reason to like the Quarter Moon Chair, only two chairs were close enough to be within conservational range. Davecki knew she'd be choosing one of those two chairs.

He deepened his slouch and listened to her order cinnamon with milk. Karla skooshed the vacuum canister and the coffee splashed into the cup. Davecki grinned. He wasn't thinking of the case now. The woman said thanks and Davecki grinned some more. Now it was time to see if he was an egotist or a keen observer of human nature. He was betting on the latter because he believed the woman ignored him on purpose when she'd entered.

Sure enough, she walked past eleven empty chairs and chose one of the only two that, for all practical purposes, created only one option between them, conversation.

"You're going to ruin your back sitting like that," the woman said.

"You sound like my mom," Davecki answered.

"Well then she must have been a very nice lady," the lady answered.

"She was. She was," Davecki said.

They both slurped coffee. Davecki knew she was Finnish. They all had a certain accent, a certain lilt to their speech. Plus, he detected the slightest aroma of sauna. It was the subtlest fragrance of cleanliness. Davecki had memorized it well during his lengthy stays at the Bill Granlund farm in Oulu during the summers of his youth.

"I'm Patty Salomaki," the blond woman said. She was five foot something and pretty in a nordic way. White skin in the fashion of new snow rather than fine china. She was forty something. Her pouty lips were red with bright lipstick.

"You don't get such nice names anymore," Davecki said."

"Why thank you Detective."

Davecki wanted to jump up and run out. She knew him as a cop and therefore had an agenda. Maybe Cancun *was* the only place where he could get away from it all.

"Oh did I say the wrong thing?" Salomaki asked.

Davecki started working on his breathing. He thought of calm water on the Big Pond. "You're a reporter."

"How perceptive," she said opening her purse and extracting a business card.

The card was a vertical jobby. On the left a majestic red pine rose from the bottom to the top in delicate greens on a blue background. All along the watchtower, no, that was Jimmi Hendrix. All along the right was the vital information. Patty Salomaki, KPUK NEWS. Davecki thought of the several jokes about the station's call letters and stuck the card in the inside pocket of his bomber.

"So, what can I do for you ma'am?" Davecki said. He sat up a little straighter.

"I was wondering if you could tell me anything about a murder that happened about ten years ago."

"There were lots of murders then," Davecki said.

"The one I'm thinking about involved a Cadillac on the anchor chain of the Anderson," Salomaki said.

Davecki knew of the case. In fact, it was rumored to involve Nick Navarone. "I don't know a lot about it," He said, "It was a Duluth case and all I can tell you is what I've heard from the rumor-mill."

"That's fair enough. What do you know? I'm thinking of doing a story on it. An exposé."

"You're asking the wrong guy. Anything I have, you can't quote. It won't do you much good, but I'll tell you what I know," Davecki said. He sat up and took a big gulp. The coffee was getting cold.

"Just consider it deep background. Completely off the record," Salomaki said.

"I've heard that before."

"And it wasn't true?"

Davecki snorted a derisive blast of air from his nostrils to cleanse his nose of one of the three great lies. He started talking. "About twenty years ago a couple of lovers vanished. Everyone thought they had run away together, thought they'd taken off to start a new life for themselves. There was some thought of foul play at the time and there were some unexplained tracks down on Port Authority land. Someone reported tracks leading to the edge of the warf and a broken guardrail. The Duluth cops sent a diver down but nothing was found. The whole thing was forgotten. Then ten years to the day after the incident, the Anderson was dragging anchor chain in a high wind as it waited for a berth at the Mesabi Docks. Low and behold, when the Anderson weighed anchor, up came a Fleetwood with two bodies in it."

"The missing lovers." Salomaki stated.

"The very," Davecki said.

"And..." she said.

"And that's that. End of story," Davecki said.

Salomaki fidgeted and said, "What? Didn't it.. I mean, wasn't there an investigation, a connection to the..."

"Of course there was," Davecki interrupted. "Everyone involved figured out the connection right away. But what could anyone do? It was ten years. There was nothing to go on..."

"That's baloney," Salomaki said.

"Well, unbaloney me," Davecki said. He sat up straight.

Salomaki straightened her hair. "What I've heard is that it was Nick Navarone's girlfriend in the car. That he had her killed because she had fallen in love with another man."

"Interesting," Davecki said.

"I heard he was so mad that he had a couple of his goons kill them both, put them in the Caddy and send them to the bottom of the bay."

Davecki started getting himself out of the booth. He was getting stiff from the badness of his good posture. "Interesting. I've heard similar talk. But, one thing's for sure, it'll never be solved. It'll always be an open case."

"Don't be too sure Detective."

"Oh?" Davecki said.

"Someone out there knows what happened. I'm going to send the case to *Unsolved Mysteries*. Maybe they'll run a segment on it and someone that's not from around here will come forward with new evidence."

"They won't live long if they do," Davecki said as he started to leave.

"Well maybe they won't care anymore. It's been a long time," Salomaki said.

"Someone will always care. They might not be very caring," Davecki said.

"I'm still going to send it in," Salomaki said.

"Knock yourself out," Davecki said as he bussed his cup. He walked away from the fiesty Finn and wondered how the term for a quick kiss had also become a description of clearing tables.

"Nice to meet you," Davecki said as he headed for the door. "Don't quote me on any of this."

"I never reveal my sources," she said.

I'll bet, he thought. "Thanks for the interesting chat," he said and escaped. He walked quickly to the Mustang and jumped in. He turned the key and looked at the dashboard clock. There was just time to stop at the grocery store and get a box of Little Debbie's to bring to the Chief. Davecki would need the treats for his boss, because he had no idea of the shit storm that was about to hit him.

21

"**D**avecki, you numb-nutted, pencil-dicked, pea-brained, stupid fucking Pollock!" Callahan screeched as the weary detective entered the Chief's office.

"Nice to see you, too," Davecki said taking a chair.

"Don't give me your smart-ass-routine fuck head. Your entire career is on the god-damn line here, mister."

"I'm mostly Irish you know, with a lot of Indian and some Croat thrown in."

"Shut the fuck up. If you want to live you cocksucker, just shut the fuck up and don't say another mother-fucking word."

Davecki wanted to tell the raging bull about the department of redundancy department but, as the Chief had brought his mother into the discussion, he figured there might be more to this than the usual vent and purge routine.

"Well?" The Chief said. His massive chest was heaving.

Something had him super-pissed, Davecki thought. "Well, what?"

"I told you not to get cute with me!"

"Sir, I'm far from cute. If you'd ask the question, I'll answer as clearly as I can."

"You have no idea?"

Davecki stared at the calming copper.

Callahan scratched his ear. "That fucking Robby Rosenrants! He said you told him about the body in the barrel."

"I did. And the name is Rosenstern," Davecki said.

"Rosencrantz? Guildenstern? Who gives a good God damn? What I want to know is why in the fucking name of God's green earth did you do such a jerk-off thing?"

"It was off the record sir. I assumed he wouldn't share the information with anyone."

"Well, if my aunt had balls she'd be my uncle, Davecki. You are off the case. Off the fucking case. That's it. I'm sick and tired of your attitude, your sloppy police work, your smart mouth, everything. I'm taking you off, giving them Kingsley.

"What are you talking about, BD? I'm not on any other case than Gronsby."

"DPD asked me to loan you to the Body in the Barrel case. Now all of a sudden the unwashed masses of Superior are acceptable to them. Well, you're not getting it. I'm going to absolutely turn it down and give 'em Joe Kingsley. He can keep his god damn mouth shut."

"BD, I never was much for working with the high priced spread over there. Do you know their starting pay is almost double ours? I don't *want* to be loaned out."

The Chief's temperature was going down. Davecki saw the bulging carotids vanishing from the bull neck as Callahan stopped pacing, pulled out his high backed executive chair and flumped himself down. The two men sat in silence. Davecki remembered the first time he met Callahan. It was the first month of the new Chief's job in Soup Town. It was also the first murder of the new guy's watch. It turned out to be the case of the not-murder. Michael Fisher, paperboy, found dead near Hill Avenue. More misinformation than a Senate confirmation hearing. Kid turned up missing. His sister found his paper wagon and mess of undelivered Tribunes near 18th and Ogden. She delivered 'em. Tin snips found in the trash behind Pete's Mobile as a possible murder weapon. Mysterious Chevy Impala found in Eagle River, Wisconsin. Many rumors about Catholic priests and a "sort of" confession from the kid's father. No conviction. Davecki was tempted to recite an Our Father for the boy, but the Chief's profanity still so tainted the air he demured.

The Chief twisted a paper clip. He looked up at Davecki without raising his head. The effect was that he was looking through his moderately bushy eyebrows. "You are one lucky S.O.B., you know that? For some reason I really, really want your badge right now. You talk to any other reporters lately?"

"You're welcome to it," Davecki fished his shield out of the bomber and tossed it at the boss. "I had lunch with some chick from Kay-puke," he added twisting the story enough to get the Chief's blood pressure reversed.

"Absolutely fucking amazing. I suppose you told her everything too?"

"All except the part about how much you loved your work and treated your cops with such respect and dignity."

"Shut the fuck up."

"Oh and we also discussed whether our society was mammo-centric or phallo-centric and who was to blame...."

"Cut it out, Dave."

"Is that an order, sir?"

"Yes."

"Then I'm not fired?"

"Go away asshole. Go catch bad guys."

"There are no bad guys anymore, sir. There are only persons of dysfunction. And, if you're giving me a direct order, I will gladly go and kick some order into the nearest dysfunctional ass I can locate."

The Chief finally smiled. "You sure are a smart mouthed little dweeb."

"Thank you sir. Can I have my badge?"

Callahan picked up the shield. He spun it with his fingers. "Maybe."

Oh oh, Davecki thought.

The shield and its leather wallet holder twirled a little faster. "I want you to take tomorrow off and go to St. Paul. Talk to Akmed's sister. Find out if her old man knew of any other errant barrels that joined the Honeywell flock."

"On my own time?"

"Well, if you don't have that urgent uncancellable appointment in the Twin Cities to go to, then you'll just have to spend the day with those Duluth guys."

"Got it. Why not just talk to her husband?"

"He's dead."

"Oh great. What happened?"

"Ran his truck into the Saint Croix River and drowned."

Davecki looked at the Jarvis print on the Chief's wall. "And how do we know these things?"

"My old buddy Nick told me."

Davecki looked back at the Chief. A chill started in his toes. It was heading north. "Navarone?"

"None other."

"Jesus, Chief. What's going on?"

"Hey, I worked the mean streets of the Minny-Apple at the time when the city was doing its best to earn the title of Murderapolis. Navarone was just a loading dock guy who could supply reliable information."

"He doesn't look like a dock dope now."

"He isn't. He never was," the Chief said. He stopped fiddling with the badge and tossed it to Davecki. He leaned back in his chair. It squeaked. "He was smart. Worked his way up fast. Got into management and like magic owned majority interest in North Bay Trucking."

Davecki, having returned the shield to its pocket said, "Then he moved the operation to Duluth, ran for office, made another fortune in politics and quit before the Mike Wallace crowd starting hounding the hucksters?"

"That's about it."

"Except?" Davecki asked.

Callahan looked through his eyebrows again. He picked up the paper clip, wrenched it apart. He looked out his window. He stared at the abandoned micro-wave tower above the Ameritech Building.

"One of Navarone's big breaks was getting the

bid on hauling barrels from Honeywell to Duluth."

"Interesting. Now exactly why do I have to do this on my day off?"

The Chief glanced at Davecki. "Well, you wouldn't exactly be going down there with my blessing."

"And that would be because...?"

"You ask too damn many questions, Davecki."

"That's my job."

"Well ask the raghead's sister. Not me."

"Anything you say, boss," Davecki said. He stood to leave, paused and asked, "Just how long did Navarone serve as Lieutenant Governor?"

Callahan shot another glance at Davecki. "He resigned after six weeks. Didn't you read back then?"

"I heard it was for personal reasons," Davecki said walking toward the door. He reached for the silver latch. He paused before pushing it down. He looked at Callahan.

The Chief was smiling and looking out the window. "He told me me personally it was, by far, the most expensive piece of ass he ever paid for. Have a nice trip," The bulky boss said without taking his eyes off the phallic object two blocks away.

22

Davecki was glad for the chance to get away. The visit to Nancy's Nook, though helpful, wasn't the same as putting some geography past your tires. He did his best thinking on the road. The Mustang climbed up Thompson Hill strong, like the good horsey it was. Davecki reached to the cassette mouth and fingered the tape in. Gregorian chants came out of the speakers. By the time he zipped under the DM & IR trestle he knew it wasn't the right music. He punched eject and drove around the hillside. He never looked back here because he knew when he returned the spectacular view would be like landing in an airplane, and he hated looking back now. It spoiled the present and tainted the future.

As he sped past the Spirit Mountain exit, he touched cruise and watched the needle settle on seventy-two miles an hour. He knew it was at the upper edge of the trooper's tolerance zone, but felt safe unless someone in a purple uniform was having a bad day.

As he steered along, Davecki thought about how freeway driving couldn't legitimately be called driving, but he was glad for the two plus hours ahead of him. It would be thinking time. Relaxing time. Reviewing time.

On the right, the Apostolic Church of Nopeming seemed to be the moving object as the car hummed along. As he descended the hill into Esko, the land of swamps and left-handed Finns, he began his recital of vitals. One: Gronsby dead. Two: ragheads didn't do it. Three: body in the barrel. Four: say no more.

So the case was just like this trip, Davecki thought, at the point where time and circumstance had to evolve. For the time being, Davecki knew he had to be patient and not speculate too much. He'd made many a bad decision in the past because he'd done too much thinking. "Our Father... Ow! Er? Father," he said out loud and tapped the steering wheel twice.

By the time Davecki finished the prayer he was going past the Black Bear Casino. Maybe I should go to Red Cliff anyway? Davecki said to himself as he resisted the urge to take the 210 exit and pay his taxes at the blackjack tables. Too tenuous, a waste of time, his inner counselor answered.

What about Hazel Cheney? She was actually at the crime scene. No way, his guts replied. No motive. She loved Gronsby. Besides her dog was named Puddles. No one could so name a dog and kill in cold blood.

Nick Navarone? Not a chance. Could be involved but way too classy to wrap a guy in a net and heave him into the big sea shining waters. But Navarone had goons who would do the bosses bidding.

The plutonium hunters weren't suspects. The body in the barrel was thirty-five years dead so it couldn't be connected. Davecki found himself gliding past the Moose Lake exit when the thought struck him. Maybe the barrel man wasn't so old. Maybe the killer or killers had dumped the barrel much more recently.

Davecki reached into the bomber, pushed the

phone aside, pulled out a pad of paper that said Arrowhead Printing on it. He put the square block of paper on his leg and wrote, TALK CHUCK ANY RECENT DUMPING? He was hoping Chuckson had seen, or had talked to a guy who heard someone say they'd seen some boat out on the lake dumping something overboard. After the scrawl, he scribbled L.S. for long shot. But it was worth a try.

Davecki wondered how far it was to Toby's. He never stopped there. He went to Cassidy's for his cinnamon roll, but he always wondered how far it was. He rarely drove to the Twin Cities; he was unfamiliar with the intervals. He passed a sign that said GAS - FOOD - LODGING EXIT 208 and wondered why the state was advertising for the Red Oak Inn. As the Sturgeon Lake exit passed, he focused on what he would ask Amal Anderson, Akmed's sister. "Excuse me for asking ma'am, but did you and your husband ever stuff a man in a barrel and drive him to the lake?" Davecki laughed and knew it was time for tunes.

He reached over and pulled the chant cassette out. He flung the audio artifact to the rider's seat and fished the Loons out of the consul below his elbow. He inserted the cassette and a woman's beautiful voice sang, "Sing me a Chippewa story under the quarter moon...." It was time to stop thinking, time to let the case develop of its own accord and, more importantly, time to veg-out until it was pastry central in Hinkley.

Davecki snapped out of his baked-goods-induced-coma when the sign above the freeway triggered some automatic alarm. Highway Thirty-six the sign said.

Mike Savage

He knew he needed that exit to get to Roseville and the suburban home of Ms. Amal Anderson. He accelerated into the left exit and sped toward county highway B. He took the Rice Street exit and thought of Jerry Rice catching footballs. He wanted to be as good as Rice at something. Before he died he wanted to be so good.

The house was green. It had old style windows, a detached garage and plenty of lawn on a corner lot. The door was white. He knocked. He stepped back. When he first started cop work, he was amazed by the other cops. They never retreated from the door after knocking. In the farm country culture where he grew up, Davecki had learned that it was impolite to impose on a door opener. The rule was, knock and step back so the host could evaluate you from a safer distance.

It was a typically bright July day. As usual, the humidity was much higher in the Twin Cities. Davecki could never figure out why anyone would want to live in such a silly city. For some reason, Davecki was expecting a tall woman, thin with long black hair, dark skin and a red dot painted on her forehead. Wrong religion he knew, and he realized just how powerful the mind can be when he experienced disappointment at the short fat lady who let him in. She did have dark skin and black hair. She did not look like Akmed in any way that he could detect. "I've been expecting you officer. You're late."

"Took the wrong Thirty-five. Do it all the time," Davecki explained.

Something in the Water

"East or west, it doesn't matter, we're halfway between both," Anderson said.

We? Davecki thought as the pudgy woman led him through a sunken living room and around two recliners facing a large screen TV and up into another living room area. Anderson pointed to a love seat beyond two more recliners that faced away from him. As he circled for the love seat, Anderson sat down on the near chair and spoke up, "This is my solicitor, Daise' Pascal."

Davecki sat at the same time a pleasant voice came from the second chair. He saw another dark haired woman smiling at him. She was young and fair skinned and looked like she was from Portugal. She also looked, Davecki thought, like Chelsea Clinton.

Davecki wondered how Chelsea liked it now that her old man was an ex-president and he wondered if the rock group fared well and he knew he was streaming at this consciousness and needed to say something. "Pleased to meet you."

The lawyer said, "Nice to meet you." Her smile was brightened by her twinkling eyes. "Is my aunt a suspect?"

Wow! Davecki thought. These people stick together. "No! Not at all! I assure you I'm simply here to ask a few questions. Though I am sorry about your brother," Davecki said switching his gaze to Amal.

"Allah works in mysterious ways," she said.

"Indeed. Inshalla Outshalla," Davecki said.

The two women exchanged glances. Davecki fetched his note pad, flipped the Chuckson page over the top and said, "Your husband was Arvid Andrew Anderson?"

Anderson looked at Daise' who nodded. "Yes," the round faced woman of sixty-something said.

"He drove truck for North Bay Trucking when the barrels were shipped to Duluth?"

"Yes."

"You told your brother there was plutonium available inside the U.S.?"

Silence.

Davecki, who had been pretending to write notes, looked up. The women were staring at each other. "My aunt, er client, declines to answer that," Pascal said.

"Err...right. I'm sorry. Too direct. Let me explain," Davecki said. "I'm out of my jurisdiction and I'm not working on any national security issues. I'm just trying to solve a local murder and am, really, quite truthfully grasping at straws by even being here. Haven't the INS boys —er, and girls— been here along with the FBI already?"

"Why yes, but..." Anderson started talking.

"Hush," Pascal said as she reached a hand over to her auntie's arm and patted it. "We'll answer questions about non-plutonium issues only," the lawyer said.

"Right," Davecki said. "My mistake."

An antique oak school clock ticked on the wall as Davecki paused long enough to breathe just a little bit deeper. He envisioned Lake Superior waves crashing to the north pier of the Duluth entry. The women sat silently. Pascal did not remove her hand from Anderson's arm. He wanted to ask, "Any idea who the dead man in the barrel is?" Instead he asked, "Did your husband have knowledge of any *other* barrels joining the Honeywell shipments? Did he, or you, ever have any contact with non-radioact...er, well, ahem. I seem to be unable to get this out without..."

"Mr. Davecki. My husband was just a truck driver providing for his family and my parents back home in Bagdad. He just did what Mr. Navarone told him. He drove to Chillicothe, Ohio, picked up some barrels, added them to the ones he was already hauling to Duluth. Mr. Navarone is the one you should be interrogating."

Interrogating. Interesting word choice, Davecki thought. He recalled the scene with Faisal in the City/County complex and thought, now that's interrogating. "I see." Davecki said and made some hen scratches on his paper.

"Ummmm," he added and wrote actual words, "Innagodda davida baby don't chew know that I love you." I wonder if that song had anything to do with the Bahagavad Gita, Davecki thought. "So," he continued, "I'm sorry. I'm feeling like a fish out of water here," he said. He saw the biggest wave in the history of western Lake Superior crash onto and topple the north phallus of the Duluth entry and said, "Any idea who the dead man in the barrel is?"

They looked at each other. Pascal nodded. Amal said, "No."

Silence reigned. The clock ticked.

"That's it?"

"Yes," said Pascal.

"Anything you remember from back then that seemed strange or might help me here?"

"We're under no obligation to help you officer," Daise' said.

"I know that and I'm sorry to have wasted your time," Davecki said. He stood up. Both women stood. As they walked toward the exit, Davecki asked, "How long did your husband work for Navarone?"

"Arvid never actually worked for him. He was employed by North Bay Trucking which was owned by Geno Gamagucci. Navarone was just a dispatcher at the time. He gave out trips and coordinated back-hauls. After the barrels contract was over Navarone bought out Gamagucci and sold off the company's assets. Sold it down to a few trucks and laid off all 280 drivers before moving the business to Duluth," Anderson said.

"That's when Arv couldn't find work and started drinking," Pascal picked up the narrative. "He ended up getting killed by some thugs at a poker game. He'd gambled away their life savings. If it weren't for the life insurance, Auntie would have lost the house."

Davecki had already opened the door and was standing quietly on the threshold. "I'm sorry," he said. "Thank you." He smiled and pulled the door shut behind him. The air conditioner in the wall came on as he trudged across the lawn. I thought old Arv drove his truck into the St. Croix, Davecki said to himself as he wiped sweat from his tall forehead. Insurance scam? He waited until he was a block away before he dialed his cellular. The phone was roaming as he made a mental note. It was one he didn't have to write down. He wouldn't forget that, one Nick Navarone, dispatcher, seemed to be awfully well financed if he could buy a 280 employee trucking company. He'd heard of leveraged buy-outs and there was probably a good explanation, but it struck him as unusual.

The phone call stopped rambling. "Hi honey. I'm on my way. I'll be there in fifteen minutes," he said cheerfully.

23

Davecki didn't mind driving in the big city. He just wouldn't live there. It was not a place that met his needs well. Having grown up in the country and on the shore of Lake Superior, he needed a higher grass to graffiti ratio to feel comfortable. The Metro Plex of St. Paul/Minneapolis did grant him one major blessing. It sheltered his daughter.

As Davecki drove up to Cossetta's Restaurant on Seventh Avenue, he was smiling. As he backed into a parking spot, he remembered the phone call of five years ago. "Is this Alphonse Davecki?" The woman's voice had asked. Not only did the voice sound hard to him, he was instantly wary whenever anyone used Alphonse. Few people knew his real name.

"Yes," he said in his cop-voice.

The hard voice hesitated. Davecki listened for clues from the background noise. There was a sort of cluttered hum he could not place. The woman's voice said, "My name is Bethany Johnson and I'm your daughter."

Davecki laughed out loud at the memory as he closed the Stang's door and twisted the key in the lock. In Superior, I wouldn't be locking down he thought. Davecki walked toward the restaurant and got comfortable with his feeling of inadequacy. He hated to admit that cities intimidated him. He found it easier to admit the prospect of fatherhood downright scared him. When Bethany announced his paternity, he felt frightened to the core and insecure. When the blood

Something in the Water

tests and DNA matched, he felt inadequate. He grew out of the shock, but not the inadequacy. Every time he met Bethany, he felt awestruck at God's ability to make life make sense, which, of course, was another source of his insecurity.

He took a tray, got in line, selected a fine looking slab of lasagna, got coffee, paid the illegal immigrant working the register, found a seat, started eating and returned to the thing he loved the most: thinking.

Bethany would arrive from her job at the Pioneer Mess over on Cedar. He wanted to enjoy his memories. Five years ago, over the course of four phone calls, he learned that Bethany's mother had gotten a baby while on summer vacation in Cornucopia. The usual adoption routine followed. Twenty three years later when Bethany had graduated from the School of Journalism at the Main U, gotten a job with the newspaper and felt strong enough emotionally, she searched out her birth parents. Davecki never knew, never suspected, never heard a word for twenty-three years. But, "yes," he said, "he did remember Belinda Bremerson," and, "no I did not know she got pregnant."

"Hi Daddy," Bethany's voice reached his ears above the din of the bistro.

Davecki looked up to see a radiant head of blaze pink hair approaching. Thick black eyebrows made stark contrast to both the wig and the light complected face.

"God I hope that's a wig," he said.

Bethany set her tray down. Spaghetti and orange pop. "Nice to see you too," she said.

174

Davecki recognized Callahan in himself and grinned at the circularity of God's ways. "Oh honey, I'm sorry. I really am. I just can't get used to how brave you are and I have to say stupid things to cover up my admiration."

"Knock it off, Davecki," Bethany said sitting. She grabbed a fork and stuffed. "Ummm," she mouthed while chewing. They both masticated and looked at each other. She swallowed first and said, "Someone squeezed the newsroom rat the other day. I knew something big would happen. I didn't think it'd be as big as plutonium barrels killing the lake and a false bottomed Iraqi freighter. And I sure didn't think it'd be you again so soon."

Before inserting food, Davecki said, "It isn't me."

"Come on Daddy. I know you're involved. You got an unsolved murder, you got the plutonium hunt going, you got a new body. Give me a break," Bethany said before pulling long and hard on the soda straw.

Capillary action, Davecki thought before answering, "It's not my jurisdiction," and "Isn't that 'got' stuff bad grammar?"

"I write better than I talk," she answered and forked in a twirl of twisted-on-the-tines pasta.

They chewed some more.

He was tempted to ask about the wig. Not.

They both drank.

She said, "How can I help?"

Davecki smiled. Like father, like daughter. "I need whatever you can find on North Bay Trucking. It was a big sled shed in the fifties and sixties before being

175

sold, downsized and moved to Duluth.

"Why?" she asked.

"If what I learned this morning is true, I have another 280 suspects."

"I thought you were out of your jurisdiction?"

Davecki sipped coffee.

"Busted?" she asked.

"Busted," he said.

Davecki told his pink-haired lady the story. She finished her soda with a loud slurping noise. The people at the next table looked and frowned. Bethany then belched loudly and turned to the yuppie control freaks with a big smile. Davecki winced and wondered if he was so obnoxious when he was young.

"I could probably get some sort of employment roster for the trucking company but it'll take some time. It seems like a waste though. Why not just bust Navarone?"

"Geeze Honey. What'd they teach you in J-school? You have to have evidence or probable cause. It's still a free country."

"Tell that to the Branch Davidians," she said.

"Right. And I should stoop to the low level of ATF and do a Janet Reno?"

She looked at him and smiled. "Can't you ever take a comment from me as a joke?"

"Oh. Heh, heh," he said.

She smiled, reached up, and pulled on her hair. The wig popped off. A cascade of luxurious brown hair fell to just below her ears. She put the wig in her lap and floofed her tresses. "There. Happy?"

"Mucho."

"What kind of evidence would you need? What should I be looking for?"

Davecki smiled. "Well, honey, who knows. Maybe one of those truckers saw something, heard something, did something that he can testify about. It's thin as ice in October, but hell, this is just procedure stuff. I'm groping. Especially when it comes to Navarone. He didn't become rich and powerful by accident. He'll never even be questioned unless there's an awfully good cause."

Bethany looked thoughtful.

"What's on your mind?"

The girl smiled. "I was just thinking of something they taught me in **J**-school," she drew out the jay and burped loudly again.

"And?"

"Behind every great fortune, there is a crime."

"So you did learn something."

"Of course. I learned enough to find you!'

"So you did. So you did."

Bethany picked the wig off her lap and played with it like it was a cat from Lewis Carroll land. "I gotta get back soon. What you gonna do next?"

"Go to the I-Max Miss bad grammar."

She sighed. "No, I mean next in the case."

"You mean the one I'm not working on?"

"Dad!"

"Can't you ever take what I say as a joke?"

She tossed the wig at him. "Touche'," she said.

He caught it and said, "I should put this on."

"Dare yah."

Davecki looked around. The restaurant was full. Every seat taken. The snobs across the isle were pretending to not look. He looked at his daughter in whom he was well pleased. "Next," he said donning the hair piece, "I'll wait for the results of the autopsy and the lab work," Davecki said straightening his new bouffant.

Bethany gasped.

"Shall we?" he said as he stood and offered his arm.

The two of them bussed their dishes and walked through the crowd being stared at by one hundred percent of the patrons. As they walked Davecki said, "You know Bethie, there's this crime lab guy named Orion...."

"Knock it off, Dad."

24

It took three weeks for the next development to occur. During that time, Davecki found himself growing increasingly impatient. One sunny afternoon he found a note on his desk. Callahan wanted to see him. After the RE: the secretary had scrawled: Gronsby.

The Chief was doing paperwork. Davecki walked in, sat down in the green chair between the door and the desk and said, "It's too nice a day for paperwork. Shouldn't you be out skimming off some graft or something fun like that?"

Callahan looked up. "Cute Dave. If I don't do this budget, you don't get paid."

"Knock yourself out Chief."

Callahan, impeccably dressed in a precise herringbone three piece suit of blue, was obviously going before the city council sometime in the very near future. The head honcho pawed through several layers of papers. He picked up a manila envelope. "Here we are," he said. "The crime lab report on the body in the barrel," he said sticking the envelope toward Davecki.

Davecki rose from his seat and plucked the paper away. "What's this got to do with Gronsby? I thought I was off the BIB case."

"You are. Kinglsey's doing just fine. Just thought you'd like to see line thirty-three," Callahan said. He folded his hands and watched.

Davecki pulled the report, turned to page two. Line thirty-three stated: "Non-uniform DNA strand *under fingernails.*" The bottom of the page was signed Orion Niroma.

"That had to be one cool mom to name her son, Orion," Davecki said.

Callahan said, "Probably some sixties hippie. What matters is the guy's the best DNA expert in the country and he's saying the guy in the barrel brought the killer's ID to the bottom."

"Why are you telling me this stuff, Chief?"

"Because I thought you'd be interested."

"AND????" He knew the Chief didn't like asking for help which is what Davecki suspected was coming. The Chief looked out his big window to the big tower across the big parking lot where his big Continental car sat. "And, as long as you're not getting anywhere with the Gronsby thing, I thought you'd like to spend some quality time with your daughter while you're tracking down the ex-employees of North Bay Trucking."

"This is bull shit Chief. You know I don't want to beat my ass all over the Twin Cities chasing down aging teamsters. It's Kingsley's job. Besides, you know Navarone's the one to talk to."

"Hey, your daughter found the roster of employees. I thought I was doing you a favor."

"Thoreau said to run and hide when you see your neighbor coming to do you a favor."

"All right already. So go. Go on, get. I've got better things to do than piss around with a worthless ingrate."

"I love you too, BD."

"Don't call me that."

"Sure thing, Chief."

Davecki stood up. As he was crossing the floor to the door Callahan said, "So, how would <u>you</u> get the powerful Nick Navarone to submit blood for a DNA test?"

Davecki stopped leaving. "That'll never happen."

"If it did, it would shorten the list of suspects by two hundred and eighty."

Davecki turned away from the door. "You think Navarone did it?"

"He's responsible even if he didn't do it. I hate it when someone gets away with murder, especially if they're rich and powerful."

"He hasn't always been rich or powerful," Davecki said.

"And he won't always be; he's going to croak like the rest of us. But, in the meantime, he is who he is and I'd like to cut him down to size if I could."

"Chief, this isn't like you. What's the deal?"

"No deal. I just don't like to waste money and manpower chasing a hoard of suspects when the prime suspect sits on his throne in the Meyer-Huff Building immune from even the most indirect questioning."

"The <u>Bible</u> says you have not because you ask not," Davecki said.

Callahan looked at Davecki. "You want to just send Kingsley in to ask the widely respected Navarone to donate blood to clear himself of a murder charge? Don't be stupid, Dave. In three minutes Tommy would be on the phone telling the Mayor I'm unemployed. She'd love to fire me *and* suck up to the governor.

"Wouldn't he *want* to clear his name?"

"Most people would. But these richy riches are touchy. They like to act offended and appalled."

"Especially if they're guilty," Davecki said.

"Especially," Callahan said. "No. What we need is a more subtle approach. Something less obvious, less attributable."

Suddenly Davecki saw it. The Chief *was* asking for help. Only he couldn't or wouldn't come right out and suggest that Davecki devise a devious and dastardly deceit to entrap the rich Italian former union operative. "Well Chief, I gotta go," Davecki said.

"Number one? Or number two, Davey?"

"Don't try to be funny, BD. It's unbecoming."

Callahan's smile vanished. "Get out, cocksucker."

"That's more like it, sir," Davecki said and left the office. He also, like Elvis, left the building. He left the parking lot in his Mustang and got on Hammond Avenue heading South. He thought about where to go. He needed time to think. He needed a while to contemplate, to free associate, to ruminate and obfuscate the obvious.

Davecki slapped the steering wheel. The destructive rhyming sequence snapped. He thought of going to the library. There was a librarian there who was a looker *and* friendly. He'd often come up with some inspired ideas in the old grocery store turned knowledge bowl on Tower Avenue.

But no, he thought there had to be somewhere else. He turned right on Twenty-first. Nancy's Nook? The place he needed would be a location where he could tell the back of his mind to solve his problem while the frontal lobes were occupied. He remembered his friend Gordy's saying, "I'd rather have a bottle in front of me than a frontal lobotomy." Coffee shop chatter would be too far into the mid-brain. No, he needed a place of solitude. He turned left on Tower. Chesapeake Bagels? No. Too sterile. He drove down Tower and wondered why it wasn't up Tower. J.W. Beecroft? No. Too many interesting booksellers and books. A speeder in a blue Escort whizzed by. He longed for the day when he could have pulled her over... hey, wait! That's the CASDA lady again. Off to kick some more abuser ass. No, I wouldn't pull her over, Davecki decided; doing too much good for the community.

The next conscious thought Davecki had was at Four Star Construction. The Johnson brothers had built a lot of righteous structures in their decades of effort. It was Dale who told Davecki about the lost locomotive of Black Lake Swamp. "They say it fell off the tracks and sank into a bottomless bog in four minutes." Dale said. Dale's cousin Dave Johnson said, "I talked to a man who said he talked to a man who knew a man that actually heard the guy describing how the locomotive sank." Now *that's* the kind of evidence that'd get a conviction, Davecki thought.

He wondered where he was going when he turned left at Greenwood Cemetery. He drove past Darrow Road Church to B. Left on B. Right at Four Corners. Left at Corbins. Maybe Anna-Gene Park? Naw, Davecki thought. Too crowded. To many swimsuits. He wound around Amnicon Lake, went left on Tri-Lakes and found County L.

Something in the Water

Something called him south. He looked left, thought of the Copper Kettle's excellent hamburger. The bartender-cook was a black haired, dark eyed beauty and he could chat up Damien the guide about the current state of steelhead fishing on the Brule.

He looked right. Something south was calling him.

He sat at the corner. The Mustang idled patiently. It was like he had gotten this far without being awake. Were those fancy houses along Amnicon Lake still there? What about Old Man Ross' machine shed? Was that there when he drove by?

Then like a drop of super glue touching his finger and thumb, the calling from the south adhered to his consciousness in an instant bond and the befuddled detective knew exactly where he was going. He let out the clutch with assurance, spun the wheel right and whacked the wheel four times. The dash rattled and Davecki smiled. He was heading to his secret place.

There was only one place in all of Northern Wisconsin that still had a grove of honest-to-goodness virgin pine. He'd learned about the location from a wise old forester who took him there to show him what the woods were like three hundred years ago.

The place didn't call to Davecki very often. But he drove now without wandering. He spent the next fifty minutes taking turns with surety and let his frontal lobes do the navigating while his occipital region did the base reasoning the primal brain was proud of. Navarone would be toast if Davecki could just keep his consciousness from intruding on the solution the brain stem was working on.

He parked the car and walked down the blacktop for four minutes. He listened to the water running in the ditch and listened for cars coming. Hardly anyone knew about this secret place. The forester didn't want more people to know about it. Davecki didn't want a car load of tourists seeing him plunge into the brush, or, worse, stop and ask him what was up. The forester had asked him to keep its location quiet. "Ten acres of three hundred-year-old pines wouldn't hold up long if half the country found out about it and started crashing around the ecosystem acting like stupid tourists," the wise old owl said.

Hearing no traffic, Davecki jumped the ditch and plunged into the alder and dogwood bushes. He pushed aside low hanging cedar limbs and walked twenty yards off the road. Then his soul exhaled. He was in a different world now. In a different time.

The trees were huge. The air was damp and still. The light was subdued. High, high above, the tops of white pine trees were shielding the direct sunlight. Had to be a hundred and fifty or two hundred feet up, Davecki thought as he craned his neck upward. Limbs. Limbs of trees everywhere. Some of the limbs could apply for, and be granted, tree status in and of themselves. Davecki looked down. Moss. Everywhere there was moss. On the forest floor beneath his feet, on tree trunks, on limbs hanging low. The sound. It was like a radio studio. All the surfaces here seemed to be capable of hearing, absorbing sound.

It was a sacred place.

Davecki wandered around the ten acres looking

for a spot. He climbed over a fallen giant tree. It took a lot of effort to get up on it and then he was high off the ground. He walked along the trunk like he was on a sidewalk. He took thirty steps before he came to branches. Then he reached out and shook hands with the first limbs. He thought about how old the limbs were. Over three hundred years ago, the hand shake would have taken place as Davecki kneeled in the wet moss in search of a tiny seedling no taller than a Bic pen stuck in the soil.

It was an awe inspiring place.

Davecki found the going difficult the further along the tree-top he walked. The apex of the tree had broken off and was bent back like a compound fracture. The acute angle of the bole wrapped around a smaller red pine and created a nearly impenetrable tangle of brush and limbs and trunk. It seemed to Davecki to be designed to keep people —him— out.

Only trouble was, the calling that had gotten him this far was coming from within the tangle. Like Thoreau submerging himself into the swamp up to his eyeballs, Davecki insinuated himself into the space. He twisted his own trunk, threaded his own limbs, unhooked his bomber from snags, bent forward, bent sideways and backwards, and, finally, found a place to sit where his butt was on dry detritus. He leaned back against the four foot thick red pine and rested his elbows on two limbs of the fallen giant.

Of course the first thing he wanted to do was leave. Then he felt the urge to pee. Then he wanted to experiment with his cell phone to see if it would work in this low spot in the terrain. He struggled to reach into the tumor-maker and punch the power key to shut the device off. Then he settled in and started on his Our Father. He made it to, "be Thy Name" before be wanted some french fries and a gyros at Louis' Cafe. He focused on his breath. He sucked in air. Pine scent. Dank taste of swamp. He envisioned the nearby river flowing quietly. He saw the black water flowing like a solid-silent-trunk of water. The river was a forty mile long tree growing south out of Lake Superior. It's tributaries were limbs, not reaching out to the sky, but stretching into the hills trying to feel up the earth.

"Our Father," Davecki said aloud. Then he gave thanks for the trees. "How can I get Navarone?" Davecki asked his Higher Power. "Should I even try?"

Then Davecki fell asleep. He dreamt he was nursing a baby. He dreamt he was breathing under water. He dreamt he was body surfing in the Pacific. He dreamt he was flying without an airplane. He dreamt he was burrowing underground, digging with his fingers through dank rich soil.

He awoke with a start. It was totally dark! Panic exploded in his gut like a letter from Ted Kaczynski. He sucked air like a black hole inhaling planets and suns.

Then he remembered where he was.

He forced himself to calm down. He sat very, very still. In the distance, he could hear peeper frogs. He reminded himself that beyond the total darkness there were stars and cars and other human beings, waitresses who could serve him a heaping plate of turkey casserole for less than four dollars. He knew he could get himself out of the tangle the same way he'd gotten in, one movement at time, one step at a time, recreate his moves into the pine grove in reverse. Davecki worked at lengthening and deepening his breaths. He took himself —mentally— back along the fallen tree trunk. He carefully envisioned every step of his inbound journey in minute detail before deciding to venture from his spot. It would be better to sit all night than get lost in one hundred and eighty-five thousand acres of state swampland. But, if he could hold his mental course, he felt he could get out without dying.

And Davecki really, really wanted to get out without dying. He was highly motivated now because his brain stem had done its job. A package had been delivered by Bill the Shakespeare quoting UPS man. It had arrived during his sleep and, when he awoke — even though the panic of it being dark had tried to destroy the gift— there it was, as plain as a three century old white pine, he knew how to get Navarone. Then Davecki realized he'd put his bomber over his head and that all he had to do was uncover himself to discover it was only late afternoon. There was plenty of daylight left.

In his car, he was exhilarated from the revelation, the visit to the pines, and the walk out. All Navarone had to do was be guilty. All Davecki had to do was have faith in his subconscious and be willing to break one teeny-weeny little law.

25

Davecki was already way the Hell and gone out in the middle of nowhere in southern Douglas County. He decided it would be convenient to stop at Lost Creek Home. Maybe Brooks Robertson would say something meaningful. Maybe he could pick up another clue and build up some good karma against his future nursing home time. Davecki drove straight east for many miles until he hit U.S. Highway Fifty-Three. He turned right. For almost twenty minutes he drove while listening to Jacqui Jaques on the radio. Davecki had met the radio personality once at a car show. She was becoming too well known for his needs. Though she would probably be willing to do what he had in mind it was ludicrous to even consider asking her. Davecki had liked the word ludicrous ever since grade school, ever since his friend told him about the word. "Just call me L.L.," Tommy Ludak had said. Though Ludicrous Ludak, as a nickname lasted only a day, the word imbedded itself like a wood tick in Davecki's mind.

Davecki turned into the long driveway at Lost Creek, saw the building, thought of Jack Nicholson and the Shining, wondered where George and Theresa were and snorted out loud. No, he'd be a fool to involve someone like Terry in his plan. Hell, he mused, he was a fool to involve *himself* in this plan. He parked the Stang, got to the third floor without being seen by Melissa or anyone who would stop him or say, "Hi." He found Brooks Robertson's room and walked in on the sound of voices beyond the drawn green curtain. He cleared his throat. The voices stopped. The curtain rattled and started south. As it turned the corner of its overhead track to the east, the hand that was pushing the drape appeared. It was feminine. It had numerous rings on the fingers. The hand bone was connected to an arm bone which led to a white sweater sleeve bunched up at an elbow. As the curtain retreated, the person connected to the elbow appeared. It was Hazel Cheney. Davecki wondered if she had any connection to Cheney Lake that great bass lake in section 14 of southern Douglas County.

The CNA looked at the cop. "What do you want?"

Crabby, thought Davecki. "Just happened by and thought I'd see how Brooksie was doing."

"People don't 'happen by' Lost Creek, Mr. Davecki. They always come for a reason."

"Isn't that true of everyone?" Davecki asked.

"**You've got a visitor Brooksie,**" Cheney hollered.

Why do young people do that to old people? Davecki thought. Brooksie, his blond hair hanging straight to the middle of his ear, looked like a young boy. Unusual haircut, stylish. Maybe they did take extra good care here he thought.

"Hey, Mr. Robertson," Davecki said, walking past Cheney to the bed where the old man sat. Large old fashioned shoes were on the floor next to the old codger's cotton sock clad feet. He had huge feet. Probably had a long marriage too, Davecki thought.

"Mr. Copper Man," Robertson said. "Keeping the Big Lady safe for all," the man said in a sort of song-chant.

"No more radiant waters, Mr. Robertson," Davecki said. He smiled.

"Call me Brooksie."

"So Brooksie, what do you know about Nick Navarone?"

"Whoo, whooo...?" Robertson began to ask.

"Nick Navarone the..." Davecki interrupted.

Robertson kicked his feet and waved a dismissing hand at Davecki.

"Don't interrupt him," Cheney said. She gave Davecki a modified *Look of Death.*

Davecki knew the many stages of the *Look of Death.* It had been used liberally in his youth to control him. He was about to apologize to Robertson when the old man spoke.

"Whoo-lee-oh," Robertson said.

"Huh? Davecki said.

"Whoo—lee-oh was the boss. He made the money. He ran the show. He took the cake. He tugged the boat, made it all float."

Davecki tried to imagine what was going on in the mind of Brooks Robertson. All he could see was a long set of railroad tracks with sections of rail missing. Robertson's feet were dancing. He started waving his arms.

"You're upsetting him. Leave," Cheney said.

Davecki remembered the lost locomotive of Black Lake Swamp, felt a great sadness, and started to leave. He felt a massive hand grip his arm. "Get 'em Copper Boy," Robertson said.

"Will do," Davecki answered. He walked out of

room 326 and willfully inhaled a long breath. Even though he didn't like the scent of nursing home, he needed to breathe away his sadness.

Next to him, as he retreated down the west wing, Hazel Cheney walked. "When he first came here, he talked better and he talked more. He often talked about his tug boat days. Several times we chatted about Navarone."

"What'd he say?"

Cheney turned left with Davecki. "Brooksie calls Navarone Julio. Said all the big guy's best buddies called him that. What else? Let's see. Big time union guy. Showed up in Duluth thirty years ago with a lot of family money and started living big. Had a way of living wild and not getting burned for it the way normal people do."

"How so?" Davecki said punching the elevator button. The light didn't come on, but there was a clunk from the shaft.

Cheney re-stabbed the button, "Come on light!" she said.

Really crabby, Davecki thought.

"What I mean is, little people pay for their sins. Rich folk don't."

The light didn't come on.

"What's that got to do with Navarone?" Davecki asked.

"Talk much?" Cheney said, giving out another: "Look of Death. " This one was more intense.

The elevator doors opened and Davecki wasn't sure he wanted to be in the same enclosed container with the seething woman whom he had interrogated for five hours. They both stepped forward. The doors closed and Davecki wondered if her anger would be coming out. He also wondered if the elevator was reliable or if he was doomed to being stuck between floors with the volatile vamp.

"When the hell are you going to make an arrest in Thurber's case?" Cheney blurted out as soon as the lift jerked downward.

Bingo! Davecki thought. "Well, I'm working on it. Other than yourself, there are no real suspects," he said.

"So arrest me asshole. Obviously your little interrogation and investigation hasn't incriminated me," Cheney barked.

Davecki wanted to laugh, knew better and even stifled his smile into the slightest of grins. The elevator rumbled as it descended.

Cheney sighed heavily and broke the uneasy silence, "So, Thurber wrapped himself in a gill net and jumped in the lake?"

"Could be. Anything's possible."

"Don't be ridiculous," Cheney said as the elevator light flashed on the square with the number one in it. Only, the elevator didn't stop. "Fucking thing!" Cheney yelled and attacked the button with her index finger.

The elevator kept trudging downward with it's peculiar little rumble that vibrated the soles of Davecki's feet. Cheney gave up on the button, folded her hands behind her back, lowered her head and stood still. She reminded Davecki of a nun praying.

The doors opened. Maybe she's got the power, Davecki thought. She didn't say a word, she just exited quickly and turned to the left.

Davecki stuck his head out of the doors and peered both ways. It looked like a kitchen beyond the bounding behind of the departing Cheney. To the right was a long hall that ended in closed double doors. Halfway down the hall was another door on the left. Above this portal, a sign hung. It said, Beauty Salon. Davecki thought of the first day of the investigation, how he'd planned on getting a haircut. He thought of Brooksie's do. The elevator doors started to close and he jumped into the hallway and started for the salon.

The door was closed. He thought about turning around. There was a large panel of frosted glass in the upper half of the door. Beyond it he could see a distorted yellow light and the shadow of a figure moving around. He was about to leave when the shadow moved quickly to the door and jerked it open.

"I knew someone was outside my door!" a purple haired woman said loudly as she eyed the startled cop intensely.

Davecki was too stunned to answer. The woman had a gold ring on every finger of both hands. Long cherry colored fingernails with sprinkles of silver imbedded in the glossy surface made Davecki want to bite down on the fingernails like they were ripe maraschino cherries. A pair of purple framed glasses hung around her neck on a gold chain.

The woman looked at Davecki for three seconds

and said, "You need a haircut." She grabbed him by the elbow and yanked him into her lair.

Davecki was steered into a turquoise cushioned chair on casters. The woman swooped a plastic apron around his neck and cinched the draw strings tight. "Comfy?" she asked as she spun the chair around and backed it up to the sink on the wall behind them.

"Urk! Arg, ummm... Sure. I'm fine," Davecki said.

The woman grabbed Davecki by the hair on the top of his head and pulled. Davecki slid down and (thank you Monty Roberts) did just what a horse would do. He leaned into the pain. The back of the chair reclined under the pressure and Davecki felt a gush of warm water cascade over his scalp.

"You know, if I was a cop I wouldn't waste my time on stupid things like murders," the woman said as she soaped up Davecki. Her fingers were strong. She attacked his hair and scalp. It reminded Davecki of a blender on puree.

"What else is there?" Davecki mumbled.

"Man, I'd go right for the graft and corruption," the woman said shooshing his hair down and up like she was a pioneer woman beating her buckskins clean on the rocks of a wilderness stream.

"Snrrg," Davecki said. He would have liked to talk, but the shampoo was numbing him. He felt like a belly-scratched labrador next to a hot wood stove after a day of duck hunting in October.

"Did you know that the Chief of Police in Superior was once called the richest police chief in the whole country?" The woman turned on the sprayer again and doused Davecki with another hypnotizing spray of luscious warm water.

"Snorggle," Davecki gargled.

"Yep, them were the days. A cop could get ahead and nobody was the worse for the wear," the woman said.

Davecki looked up at her as she hosed him down. The purple glasses bounced on her smock as she toweled him. She grabbed him by the hair again and pulled. He followed the pull and sat up.

"Name's Yvonne, Detective," the woman said as she combed his hair straight.

"Ahhh..."

"You'll find out who killed Thurber Gronsby all right," Yvonne said as she started snipping hair at a furious pace, "it's just too bad you couldn't find a trunk full of money to keep or maybe a suitcase full of diamonds! Wouldn't that be neat?!" she said snipping as if she'd just downed three straight cups of Nancy's Nook coffee.

"Ahhh,"

"You know Mr. Davecki, I've always admired your work. I especially liked that business with the Chinese guy from the Yugoslavian grain ship. That was so funny! How did you think to look in the chimney?"

Davecki wanted to tell her that five squadmen and two detectives had searched Mitsie's Massage for two hours looking for the Chinaman who'd shot his hooker in the left eye. They were about to give up when Davecki, for some reason, remembered Dave Evans, the local raptor guy who'd found a missing snowy owl in the chimney of the Androy Hotel. Sure enough, they looked in the flue of the old hotel that Mitsie had turned into a thriving massage establishment and found Mr. Wan Hong Lo huddled amongst the old coal clinkers and covered with soot and pigeon shit.

But, naturally, he couldn't say a word because Yvonne was yammering. "Well, you'll figure it out Mr. Davecki. Nick Navarone is behind all this. I can tell you that for sure. Brooksie always used to tell me stories about Navarone when I did his hair. You'll see. Navarone's behind all this," Yvonne said as she grabbed a blow dryer and turned the hot blast on Davecki's tresses.

As the roar of the hair dryer echoed in his ears, Davecki wondered who in the hell this woman was and how in the hell he'd managed to get himself into this situation. He also was hearing some sort of contrapuntal noise that seemed to be competing with the hair dryer's clammor.

"WHAT?" Yvonne yelled.

"Sure. Okay. Be right there," she shrieked and shut the dryer off. She threw it onto the counter next to the sink and said, "Gotta go fast Detective. Mrs. Steinskin's got her hair tangled in her wheelchair spokes again." Yvonne took off through the door. Halfway out she called over her shoulder, "This one's on the house, sir. If you do find a shitload of diamonds, sneak a handful out for me!"

And she was gone.

Davecki sat for a minute and considered that Dorothy must have felt just the way he was now feeling after landing in Oz. He stood and yanked the cape around. There were big blue ducks screen printed on the opaque plastic. He undid the tie, floofed his half-dry hair and looked in the mirror. "Not bad," he said. Just before he exited the room he spied a box of Little Debbie Zebra Cakes. He shook the box. The last pack fell into his palm. He figured that, as long as he was embarking on a crime spree, why not? He ripped the cellophane off and chomped down. "Yum," he said. He put the remaining cupcake in his pocket, pulled an Elvis and left the building. He felt happy that, as long as he was going to break the law, he would at least be looking good.

26

Madam Bovery answered the door. "Well, officer! To what do we owe this surprise visit?" she said loudly.

Davecki heard the shuffling of feet, imagined the vanishing act of John this and John that. "I'm not here on official business, Rose."

"Well, Dave, I didn't know."

"I'm not here for that either," Davecki said as he followed the lady of the house into the sitting room.

"Well then, why *are* you here David?"

"I need Nick Navarone's sperm," he said following the Madam inside.

Three-fourteen John had been a whorehouse since from forever. Five generations of kids whispered about it. Six generations of sailors visited the long tall building with the many windows and numerous rooms. The second floor was all bedrooms on either side of a long hall. The first floor was where Rosie and her mother paid off the gendarmes and played cribbage with Mayors from both cities and all the surrounding towns from Hinkley to Hurley, I-Falls to Chippewa Falls and points in between. The first floor was also the location of the kitchen, one of two bathrooms for the entire twenty room building, the parlor, sitting room and coat room. The basement was significant only in that it had a set of wide oak doors, put in during prohibition, to allow easy access for all the rum barrels in transit from Canada to a thirsty U.S.A.

Rose herself was a short woman. In her fifties,

she had been a beautiful girl. She grew up to be a gorgeous but abused teenager. From that hell she emerged with an unusual aplomb and an unflappable nature that catapulted her into an unequaled elegance which pretty much put everyone near her into an automatic state of obsequious submission. If her career path had been accounting, she would have become Treasurer of State or a fantastically rich CEO at a multi-national company. Her hair was brown. Her eyes were blue. She walked like an athlete. She would have been prom queen if her father would have let little Jimmy Hendricks escort her. Rosie's voice chimed like a bell when she talked and her words, though rarely harsh, were always sure. Rosie never guessed and questioned little.

"This sounds like a job for Sparky," Rose said as she lead Davecki past the sitting room toward the parlor.

Davecki looked left and saw four women sitting in various comfy chairs. Two were playing cards. They were both blond. The one with black fingernails said, "Go fish." Her partner had a row of ear rings numbering at least ten climbing up her ear. The silver loops accented the girl's close cropped hair. She reached for a card as Rosie said, "Say hello to Mr. Davecki, girls."

The two women glanced up and mumbled their hellos. The third woman was reading a slick advertorial magazine that pretended to be interested in area women but was more fixated on selling ads. This one didn't look up. The fourth woman was staring at a crossword puzzle, pen in hand. When she turned to greet the cop, both hooker and detective were surprised to see each other. It was the looker from the library. Rosie moved off toward the sitting room. Davecki followed, figuring that it probably *was* difficult to make it financially on a librarian's pay.

"So David," Rosie said entering the sitting room and plunking herself down on a finely crafted love seat that had to be eighty years old. Her fine neck length hair bounced as she sat. "I do so want to thank you for getting those dreadful barrels out of the lake."

"I was just out fishing, Rose."

"Pashaw," Rosie said. "'You the man Dave', as the young people say."

Davecki sat in a soft cushioned Victorian chair with a padded heart shaped back. "I haven't heard anyone say pashaw since my mother died."

"Well, you've been hanging with the wrong crowd," Rosie said reaching for a pack of gum on the end table. "God I wish these were cigarettes," she said pulling out a stick.

Rosie looked at him. "So, I imagine this little project of yours is going to be generously funded with capital from the police budget?"

"Right Rose, I've got the paperwork on BD's desk as we speak."

Rose smacked her lips lightly as she chewed her gum. They sat thinking, looking each other over. Rose snapped her gum between her teeth. Davecki worked at expanding his chest beyond its tightened capacity. "It probably won't work," Davecki finally said.

"She'd have to testify, have to save the evidence for some reason, have to convince a jury that she acted alone, wasn't prompted by the police. She would have to get Navarone interested and be willing to vanish after the trial." Davecki actually wrung his hands. He stood up. He sat down. His breathing wasn't going well. "It's a stupid idea."

Rose smiled. "It's not that David. It can be done. 'All that the mind of man can conceive, a man can do.' What I don't get is why?" she said.

Davecki stared. The silence seemed to want an answer so Davecki started rambling, "Because there's another body...."

"The body in the barrel..."

"Yes," Davecki said.

"Yes?...." Rose rose from the divan and said, "David you've got to relax." She walked behind Davecki's chair and started a shoulder massage. Davecki shrugged his shoulders high and cracked his clavicles loudly.

"Ugh!" Rosie said. "That sounds horrible."

"You've got strong fingers."

Rosie laughed. "From all the penny pinching I do," she said, her voice chiming again like the bells of Pilgrim Church on Belknap.

Davecki sighed. He let Rose massage. She said nothing. She let her fingers do the talking. After a few minutes Rose said, "It seems so indirect, so round about."

"Huh?" Davecki's eyes were cloudy.

"Why not just ask him?"

Davecki straightened out of the slump the massage had put him in. "I'm off the BIB case. Plus policemen can't go harassing people without cause. Especially rich people with political power who can end careers and make Cadillacs vanish for ten years."

Rose took Davecki by the hair with her left hand. She held the top of his head. She started pinching his neck.

"I feel like the top of my head could blow off."

"You remind me of the Indian who went to the psychiatrist."

"Huh?" Davecki said rotating his head slightly.

"This Indian goes to a shrink and says, 'Doc, I keep dreaming I'm in a tee pee.

"'Um-um,' the shrink says

"'And I keep dreaming I'm in a pup tent,' the Indian said.

"'I know what your problem is,' the shrink says, 'You're two tents.'" Rosie laughed, slapped Davecki on the top of his head and returned to her seat.

"Thanks Rose," Davecki said rotating his head all around and shrugging his shoulders more.

"Is there some law against you just talking to the man? I mean, can't a cop just chat a guy up? Is that police harassment?"

"There's no law against asking questions. You just gotta be careful not to badger or intimidate or act without probable cause."

Rosie reached for the gum pack. She looked at Davecki and didn't pick the condiment up. "So, if for instance you wanted to skip all that stuff about sperm...now, why did you want that?"

Davecki wished he'd never stopped at three-fourteen John. He said, "Navarone will never volunteer for a blood test so I figured a rich guy like him could be seduced and wouldn't be suspicious until it was too late. Then I could match the DNA under the fingernails of the body in the barrel with the sperm and prove that Navarone killed whoever it is in there and then connect him to Thurber's death."

"Too complicated!" Rosie laughed.

"What would you do?"

"I'd ask him myself. Get right to the point."

"Easy for you to say. I can't go over to Duluth, walk into his restaurant and ask, "Did you stuff some guy in a barrel thirty years ago?"

"What if you were to accidentally bump into him, say...in Superior somewhere?"

Davecki felt all the relaxation of Rosie's rub vanish. "He's here?"

"Should be down in a few minutes," Rose grinned.

"I'll be damned," Davecki said.

"Luck of the Irish," Rosie said.

27

Navarone walked into the sitting room. His face, before he spotted Davecki, looked happy. When the rich man's eyes fell on the cop, the face changed from soft to concrete hard in an instant.

"What the hell do you want?" Navarone said through thick lips. His face was long, his skin splotchy but surprisingly wrinkle free. He had big leathery hands that were wrinkled.

Face lift, Davecki said to himself when he noted that difference.

The rich man was also wide. He was probably an immensely strong young man. Now his shoulders were stooped. His hair was white at the temples and thin brown at the crown. It was stylishly long to the top of this ears which had no hair in them. Nair, Davecki thought remembering that his neighbor, Elmer Warbalow, at eighty, had great tufts of ear hair sprouting from his listeners. "To be honest with you, Mr. Navarone, I would like to know if you killed Thurber Gronsby and if you stuffed that body in that barrel thirty years ago."

Navarone looked at Rosie. "You've seen the last of me Rose. This used to be a class operation. Now a man can't find peace here."

"Hey. It's a free county. Anybody's welcome to find a piece here," Rosie said.

She sounds calm, Davecki thought.

"I won't dignify your question with an answer, Mr. Davecki," Navarone said. He lifted a seven hundred dollar top coat off the coat tree and draped it over his left arm. "But you will be getting a lot of time off very soon. You can count on it," he said.

"That would be nice. Rosie says I'm two tents anyway. I could use a break," Davecki said.

"You have a smart mouth young man. You could use an attitude adjustment and I think I'm the man to apply it."

Davecki was not a violent man. In fact, he often wondered how he got into law enFORCEment. But he was a man and his anger got up as he rose from the chair in response to Navarone's aggression. He looked at Rose and said, "Rosie, I'm sorry. I didn't come here to cause trouble but I'm afraid I'm going to have to arrest Mr. Navarone and yourself on charges of solicitation and prostitution."

"David! Well! I never!" Rosie said.

Davecki looked closely at her. Was she really angry or was there a hint of a smile deep in those blue eyes?

"You WILL regret this Davecki," Navarone said.

"Probably. But a man's gotta do what a man's gotta do." As Davecki spoke, a woman walked into the room from the rear of the building. She had shoulder length dark hair, and an oval face with dark eyebrows. Her nose was turned up just so nicely and her eyes were slightly crossed.

"Sparky, this is Detective Dave Davecki," Rose said.

"Nice to meet you," Sparky said coming around Navarone and extending her hand. "Am I under arrest?"

"Afraid so," Rosie said.

"Oh goodie!" Sparky squealed. "I've got to tell Josie!" and she ran out of the room. The red terry cloth robe she had on sailed behind her like Superman's cape.

Rosie smiled. "She is such a case! Now, of course you'll have to be arresting us all right?" Rosie said.

Davecki thought of the librarian. "Well...."

"Mr. Davecki, I suggest you get another job," Navarone said and he walked out.

There was a burst of shouting and general exclamations of alarm from the parlor. "I better go calm 'em down," Rose said. "Can I see you out or do you want to go upstairs?"

Davecki hadn't heard. He was staring at the space where Navarone had stood. He felt gutted. How can someone do that? Just gut you with such ease? "Huh?" Davecki said when Rosie touched his arm.

"It'll be okay honey. These things have a way of working themselves out. After all," she pulled him toward the parlor where the hubbub was still hubbubbing, "Lake Superior they say doesn't give up her dead, but it did cough up Thurber Gronsby and spit out those barrels after thirty years."

"Uh huh," Davecki said. He felt like a sheep being lead to slaughter.

As they entered the hallway between the two rooms, Davecki saw the back side of the librarian running out the front door and around a departing Navarone. Rose steered him into the parlor. "Calm down ladies!" she commanded. The two blondes were

207

still holding their cards. Sparky was grinning and tightening the tie on her robe.

"We were just having a little fun at Mr. Navarone's expense," Rosie said. "No need to panic."

"You mean I'm not going to jail? I never been arrested," Sparky said.

"She's hooked on cops," short-haired Blondie said.

"Let's finish," long Blondie said.

The two women sat down at the card table and resumed their game.

"If you're not going to arrest me, could you at least interrogate me? Maybe force a confession with one of those rubber hoses, or, what did Daddy call those things? A sap?"

I'm the sap, Davecki thought.

"Settle down, Sparky," Rose said.

"I want to be arrested. Can't he at least handcuff me?"

Rose looked at Davecki. There was a please in the look. He could see it now that it *was* fun behind her eyes, that she had been toying with Navarone.

"I suppose," Davecki said slowly.

"Oh goodie, goodie. Can you throw me into the back of a squad car? I want to be behind one of those cage thingys."

"I don't drive a squad car," Davecki said fishing in the inside pocket of his bomber for his cuffs.

"What kind of cop are you?" Sparky said.

"Go fish," Blondie said.

"He's the best kind," Rosie said.

When Davecki pulled his cuffs, Sparky stuck both

her arms out and held the wrists together. He put them around the girl's thin bones and noted that the steel bands neatly covered up the scars.

"You got to lead me away now!" Sparky trilled.

"Settle down Sparky," Close-cropped Blondie said.

"Lead me!" Sparky shrilled.

"Dave?" Rose said.

"Where? How? I can't take her in."

"Haul me away officer!" Sparky barked.

Davecki wondered if she was on drugs.

"Take her to the kitchen," Rose said. "I need a cup of tea."

"I won't resist officer," Sparky said.

"Detective," Davecki said grabbing the hooker by the elbow.

"Ooooh, you're one of those? You're one of those what-cha-ma-callets? A...a....Dick! That's it. You're a Dick aren't you?" Sparky chattered like a squirrel.

"You're a dick-head," long Blondie said.

Rose was exiting. Davecki steered his prisoner after the departing madam.

"This is so exciting!" Sparky sparkled.

"Calm down, young lady." Rose said.

"Calm down, young lady," Sparky mimicked.

Davecki sighed.

They walked past the sitting room. Davecki could smell Navarone's essence. He hated the rich man.

"I'll get some water going." Rose said. She pulled a stainless steel pot from the front burner of the gas stove and went to the sink, she twisted the knob on an antique looking faucet that stuck out of an enormous enamel sink-back that had to be a hundred years old. Water tumbled out of the nozzle in a helter-skelter spray.

Davecki thought of Lake Superior when he saw, heard and smelled the water. He was glad the aroma of the lake was replacing the stench of Navarone.

Rose pulled the red trigger under the black handle of the water kettle. The black lid popped off the pig-snouted spout. Rosie stuck the opening under the flow of water.

"I'll tell you everything you want to know, Detective. You don't have to beat me. I'll confess!" Sparky sparked.

"Pamela!" Rose said. "Settle down!"

The madam's sharp tone scared even Davecki and he felt Sparky come unglued in his hand.

"I was just having some fun," Sparky said.

Rose put the full kettle on the stove burner and twisted a large oblong knob at the front of the appliance. It, too, was very old. The legs were long and green. It looked more like a table than a stove. The black top had a sheen from decades of being cleaned and then greased up from frying foods. A halo of blue flared and settled into a devilish flutter under the water kettle like a Karner Blue butterfly attending to a Purple Loosestrife blossom.

Davecki steered Sparky to a corner seat between the red trimmed porcelain kitchen table. A pepper shaker was all that sat atop the table.

"Aren't you at least going to cuff me up?! Sparky

said. She looked so sad, disappointed that she wasn't
getting to play cops and robbers.

Davecki looked at Rose.

Rose said, "You better shake her down some officer. Give her a little going over," Rose said. She'd
adopted a play-voice.

Davecki looked at Sparky. She smiled up at him.
He recalled his black lab puppy, Lennie. He sighed.
Then he laughed. And he felt his chest muscles ease
up. There was something about the girl's face that
made him laugh. He too adopted a tone, a tough guy
tone. "All right lady. Anything you say can and will
be used against you in a court of law. You have the
right to an attorney. You have the right to remain
silent. Do you understand these rights?"

Sparky lowered her head. "I do," she said.

"Don't try to lie lady," Rose said approaching the
table. She put her strong fingered hands flat on the
table. "If you lie, my partner here will leave the room
and there's no telling what I'm capable of doing," Rose
growled.

"Oooh! Good cop, bad cop. This is fun!" Sparky
said.

Davecki felt his insides get mushy. "Listen you.
No smart mouth. Just tell us what we want to know
and I'll keep my partner here from putting her hands
on you. You don't want that," Davecki said.

Sparky looked at Rose. She looked at Davecki.
She said, "I'll tell you anything you want to know,
Detective."

Davecki was stuck. Inside himself he couldn't

find more words for the play. He was used to playing for real, not playing for fun.

Rose came to the rescue. "Just tell us who the guy in the barrel is and who killed him and we'll talk to the judge. Ask him to go easy on ya. Ain't that right, Dave?"

"Yeah. Right. Sure," Davecki said. "You'll only get twenty years for accessory murder lady," Davecki joined in.

"I don't wanna die!" Sparky cried. She cupped her face in her hands.

Davecki thought of the scars on those wrists. He felt a sense of bizarreness rise from his guts. "You ain't gonna die," he said.

"It's.....it's...." and Sparky started sobbing hard into her hands.

"Okay Sparky," Rose said. "That's enough. We were just goofing around."

But Sparky kept on sobbing. Through her hands she said, "No, it's true. I don't want to die!"

Davecki had heard enough confessions to sense that this had somehow transmogrified from play to something else. Was it real? Or was it Memorex? "What's the problem Sparky?" Davecki said glancing at Rose.

"Julio said he'd kill me if I told."

Davecki recalled what Hazel Cheney had said about Navarone's closest friends using the rich man's middle name and found Sparky's story a little more believable.

Rose went to the girl's side, put her arm around

212

her and motioned to Davecki to remove the cuffs.

Davecki pulled his keys from his pocket and reached for the hardware.

"I don't want 'em off!" Sparky yelled and jerked her hands away.

"Okay. Okay." Davecki said. "It's okay."

"What'sup honey?" Rose asked gently.

"He told me all about it and said I could never tell or he'd kill me."

"Navarone?" Davecki asked.

"Yes," Sparky sobbed.

"You can tell us honey. You got to tell us or it'll eat you alive," Rose counseled.

Just as the water kettle started to sing from the boiling water within, Sparky said, "He told me the body in the barrel was Jimmy Hoffa!"

28

I t's funny how things work out. Not funny, ha ha, but funny, odd, strange, bizarre. Davecki didn't have to decide to break the law. Navarone didn't have to visit three-fourteen John that night, didn't have to fall for a hooker. But, these strange coincidences occur constantly. There's Roswell, New Mexico. And what about Bill Clinton? He got his crooked little penis shot off didn't he? Strange indeed. Just think about the likelihood of Michael Jackson getting married or Prince Charles giving a kidney to some nut from Duluth. Strange indeed. And yet these are things that happen all the time.

So, it wasn't odd that the following day Detective Alphonse "Dave" Davecki would walk into Chief Richard "B.D." Callahan's office holding between his thumb and forefinger, a used condom with a dollop of sperm resident.

"What in the Hell?" Callahan said.

"Got an evidence bag, Chief?"

"For Christ's sake, Davecki," Callahan said yanking open a low drawer on the right side of the big desk he was sitting at. He nearly jerked the handle off he was in such a rush.

As the Chief ransacked the drawer, Davecki realized he'd come upon another nickname for his boss. "Here," Callahan said tossing the E.B. across the B.D. to D.D. The Chief threw an evidence bag across the big desk.

"Thanks B.D.," Davecki said dropping the sexual

aid into the bag. He sealed the top.

"Don't call me that."

"Sure thing Chief."

"What's going on, Davecki?"

"This is Nick Navarone's sperm," Davecki said holding the evidence high like it was the Stanley Cup. Orion Niroma at the crime lab will prove that the DNA in this bag matches the DNA under the fingernails of Jimmy Hoffa."

Callahan froze, "What?"

"What what?" Davecki said smiling.

"Who?"

"Jimmy Hoffa."

"All right, I heard you the first time. Now, tell me everything."

Davecki put the evidence on Callahan's B.D. He was about to sit when Callahan, eyeing the bag, said, "Put that on the floor."

Davecki returned to the bag, placed it on the green carpet and returned to the chair which Callahan kept too far away for Davecki's liking. He plopped down, adjusted his bomber. He fussed.

"Come on dammit," Callahan said.

Davecki said, "I'm enjoying this. Give me a break."

Callahan sighed and folded his hands.

Davecki got himself all organized in the chair and cleared this throat. "Ahem. Ahem. We got a witness that will testify that Nick Navarone killed Jimmy Hoffa thirty years ago, stuffed him in a barrel, snuck it alongside the Goodyear atomic cans and sank 'em all to the bottom of the lake.

"And who might this witness be?"

"Sparky Anderson."

"The hooker?"

"The very."

"And she just came forward as a matter of conscience?"

"I'd say that's about right."

Callahan pulled open the left drawer, fetched a big cigar and initiated the lite-up ritual. "Why'd she come to you? Or was it with you?"

"Hardly. I was at three-fourteen on official police business and she volunteered the information.

Callahan puffed.

Davecki rose. He bent to retrieve the evidence.

"Where you going? You're not done here."

"I'll come back when the air is clear. I've got to register this and get it Fed-Exed to Madison."

"Sit down dammit!"

"Hey Big Chief Second Hand Smoke. No smoking building. All that. I'll be back."

Callahan pulled the center drawer of his desk open and smashed out the cigar.

Davecki waved an arm about to dispel the smog. "Very clever place for an ashtray in a non-smoking building," he smirked. He sat down. "Sparky says that thirty-odd years ago Navarone was on the dock of North Bay Trucking one night. She says Navarone has told her this story more than once. She calls him Julio. All his closest friends do," Davecki crowed. "She says Navarone was getting a shipment of barrels ready for the lake when a big black Caddy rolls into the lot. A guy gets out and walks up to Navarone. It was, according to Sparky, Jimmy Hoffa looking for a place to hide."

Callahan interrupted. "Hoffa was alone?"

"Sparky didn't say. All she said was that Navarone said the trunk and back seat of Hoffa's Caddy was filled with boxes and bags and stacks of cash concealed beneath a Hudson's Bay blanket. She said that Navarone whacked Hoffa in the head with a frozen ten pound walleye from a Kemp's seafood shipment, barreled him, took the cash and carried on, making himself into the self-styled millionaire politician he is today."

"Hearsay. It's all hearsay. Not admissible." Callahan said. He picked up the cigar and fondled it.

"Sure. Okay," Davecki said, "But when this DNA match comes up positive, we'll have enough to arrest him and convict him of murder and attempted murder."

"Attempted murder?" Callahan asked.

"Sure, of Lake Superior!"

"What?"

"Chief, the barrels. He tried to kill the entire lake with the plutonium."

"Get real Davecki."

The detective fidgeted in his chair. "Well, at the very least, we can get him directly attached to the body in the barrel."

"So? That's no good in the Gronsby case."

Davecki fidgeted more.

Something in the Water

"What's on your mind Detective?"

"Well sir, B.D. I....Well, I was thinking, if I went over there now and confronted Navarone, made a surprise visit and announced that he was under arrest for the murder of Jimmy Hoffa, well, maybe he'd do something stupid, something rash."

"Like what? Have his goons kill you the same way they did Gronsby?"

"Get real Chief. Then he'd have to have Sparky Anderson killed. Then you'd be next. Pretty soon he's halving half the population just to keep a thirty-year-old secret ."

"Who knows what could happen? He did, after all, move to Duluth with millions in cash," Callahan said.

"You're right. That does reveal a proclivity for stupidity," Callahan said. He rolled the Cuban around in his stubby fingers. "I have a question."

"Shoot," Davecki said.

"Why'd Navarone tell his whore? I mean, there's an unknown body on the warehouse floor in Duluth. Why tell anyone? It's too risky."

"I asked Sparky the same thing. She said Navarone first told her years ago before the barrel thing ever came up."

Callahan stopped worrying the cigar. "Then along comes eco-warrior Gronsby. The barrels could come up. Navarone knows the consequences. He has his men whack Gronsby..."

The cops sat there in silence. Smoke oozed from the desk drawer.

"Your desk is on fire, chief," Davecki said.

Why didn't Navarone barrel Gronsby up?" Callahan asked as he opened the middle drawer and again smashed the stogie ashes out.

"Who knows? If you let me go arrest him, you can ask that very question yourself," Davecki said.

"Now?"

"Sure."

"No. We'll wait for the DNA tests to come back."

"Come on Chief. Navarone's not dumb. He could be in Bolivia right now. Let me confront him."

"You really want to rub those Duluth cops' noses in this don't you?"

"That would be nice. But mostly I want to rub Navarone's nose in some good old fashioned justice."

"You sure about this? It could mean our jobs." Callahan's face was red, flushed with excitement.

"I'm sure," Davecki said fidgeting.

"Okay then. Let's go arrest the bastard."

"Us? You and me?"

"Hell yes. I don't want to miss out on this for anything," the Chief said getting up. "You drive."

"Anything you say, B.D."

"Don't call me that."

"Sure thing Chief."

29

Even though visibility sucked, Davecki floored the Mustang up the Superior approach to the Highbridge. The stretch between the two cities was the best race course around. It was impossible to get caught speeding. Callahan talked to the DPD on his cell phone. It was a typical Twin Ports summer afternoon. Foggy. "But it was a nice fog." Davecki had heard that statement hundreds of times over the decades. The Big Lake was fond of enshrouding its shores with a shawl of gray. On this particular day, the mist draped lightly over the land. As the Mustang climbed toward the top of John Blatnik's bridge, the sun became more and more evident. Suddenly the fog vanished and the blue sky appeared above the superstructure of the Highbridge. Davecki shut the windshield wipers off just as Callahan flipped his phone shut.

The Chief put the phone in the inside pocket of his SPD blazer. "They're going to meet us at Glen Avon Church parking lot," he said adjusting the shoulder belt around his barrel chestedness.

Davecki said, "I remember the first time I went to Hunter's Park. I couldn't figure out why someone as rich as Navarone would stay in such a middle class neighborhood."

"Politics," Callahan said.

"Harumph," Davecki answered. He looked out to sea and saw a big laker way off toward the horizon. The fog was only near the shore. The lake had done

an incomplete job of frosting the land. The lift bridge
was sticking out of a chiffon type cloud. Enger Tower
was clearly visible. Halfway down the Central Hillside the fog-edge was indistinct and irregular. The
spire of Sacred Heart Music Center rose sharply from
the chiffon. It pointed toward heaven and Davecki
wondered why it seemed like an obscene gesture. Perhaps it was the building's way of relating after endur-
ing the threat of demolition. As the detective slowed
and wheeled his car back into the gloom that covered
Rice's Point, the last thing he saw was the antenna
farm atop the escarpment.

"It's all image you know," Callahan said as
Davecki switched on the intermittent wipers.

The Dick turned on his headlights and gave one
of his most eloquent answers ever, "Huh?"

"Yeah," Callahan said shifting in his seat, "When
you get to that level; money, power, prestige, it's all a
matter of image."

"Uh-huh," Davecki said. He slowed the car to
match the visibility. He knew from years of experience that the gopher gang liked to set speed traps on
Rice's Point. They used to run their unconstitutional
drunk driver sweeps on the southbound lane too, picking up drunks heading for Soup Town after the 12:30
bar closings in Duluth. Thank God, the legislature
wised up on that one Davecki thought.

"Take Joe Kennedy for instance," Callahan was
going on, "He was a big-time womanizer but had his
daughter lobotomized because she was too frisky. She
lives in Wisconsin you know. Did you know that
Dave?"

"Yeah, you've mentioned it once or twice."

"Smart ass," Callahan said. He closed his mouth tightly and crossed his arms.

Davecki took the northbound exit and said, "Who's going to make the pinch?"

"Oh I suppose it'll be One Nut Nelson."

"Yeah," Davecki said thinking of the Duluth Dick who arrested Toivo Brah, the organ trafficker from Embarrass.

"You know, if Brah hadn't tipped that waitress at Lake Avenue Cafe two hundred dollars he'd probably never have been caught," Davecki said.

"They always get caught," Callahan said.

The car pushed through the fog. On their right the DECC sign flashed the news that Molly Scheer was appearing on August Seventh.

"Fog's lifting," Davecki said.

"How so?"

"I had enough time to read that LeAnn Rhymes is opening for Molly," Davecki said.

Both men peered through the safety glass. The fog was vanishing at an astonishing rate. Just as the Mustang approached the Lake Avenue overpass, Davecki saw a green XJ-12 heading south toward Canal Park. "Hey!" Davecki said, "There's Navarone's car!"

"Shit," Callahan said. "You sure?"

He looked askance at his boss. "Nobody knows more about cars than Dave Davecki," he said.

"Silly me," Callahan said reaching for his phone.

Davecki grinned. "I've always wanted to do this."

He checked his rearview mirrors. He hit the brakes, pulled over to the far left and yanked the emergency brake. The Mustang started into a squealing skid and did what the laws of physics required. It swooped around to the right as Davecki counter-steered.

"God dammit Dave!" Callahan roared. The Chief was trying to hold on to the dash, the door and his phone all at the same time.

As the Mustang came around, Davecki jammed the shifter from fifth to second. At just the right moment, as the momentum of the skid diminished, Davecki released the brake handle. At the same time, he punched the accelerator and dumped the clutch. Now the Mustang, which had risked coming to a complete stop as the skid threatened to lose its juice, continued the swoop as a bona-fide power slide.

"God dammit Davecki!" Callahan said clutching at multiple smooth surfaces.

"EEEEhaw!" Davecki said pointing the nose of his horsey up the down ramp. The Detective punched the power down toggle on his window control array. He reached between his legs and pulled out his Kojak. He threw the switch. The red light started pulsing. He threw the magnetic bottomed device onto his roof and began concentrating on what lay ahead.

It was a big black Blazer first. Davecki hugged the right rail of the down ramp. He made sweeping motions to the left out the driver's side window with his left arm. The Blazer driver swerved out of harm's way and two cars behind the sport-ute followed suit. The Mustang shot out onto Lake Avenue like a silver salmon breaking water with a number three Fedo Flasher in its jaw. The last problem was the six inch tall concrete meridian between traffic lanes.

"Shit!" Callahan yelled when he saw the barrier.

"Hang on!" Davecki yelped. The Mustang hit the curb hard and jumped over at the same time as a crashing/tearing noise exploded from under the front end. "There goes my air dam," Davecki whined.

"You'll need an alignment now," Callahan said laughing. "That was fun. Can we do it again?"

"Up your's," Davecki snapped. He added, "The Department's going to pay."

"Later Dave," Callahan said with a chuckle.

Mercifully, traffic was clear. The fog had kept pedestrians off the streets and made drivers cautious. Now said fog was intermittent, blotchy, like Navarone's skin. There were huge chunks of cloud lumbering about independently like advanced stage Alzheimer patients. Davecki thought of the saying, "Don't like the weather in Duluth? Wait a few minutes." In the large spaces between the fog chunks, visibility was excellent.

Callahan was able to dial.

Davecki raced down the slanted roadway toward Canal Park.

30

"Call DPD and tell 'em we're in pursuit," Davecki ordered.

Anything you say, big guy," Callahan said poking at the phone. He hit hot-dial and said, "And how many toppings do you want on that extra large sir?"

"Very funny," Davecki said. He jammed the Mustang's shifter into third gear and stomped on the gas pedal. The car's posi-traction rear-end broke free and powered into a perfectly controlled slide. At the howl of the tires two dozen white pigeons burst out of the windows and off the ledges of the Duluth Steam Plant on the right.

Callahan planted the phone on his left ear and held onto the door handle with his right. "Yeah, this is Chief Callahan of SPD. Tell Lieutenant Kingsley and his playmates the Glenn Avon Meeting is off. We're in pursuit of the suspect, Nick Navarone, south on Lake Avenue."

Davecki scanned right for the Jaguar. The fog was splotchy. He could see all the way to the nose of the Irvin but no further. "Which way'd he go?"

"Straight," Callahan said stuffing the phone between his legs.

"Nuggie cancer there," Davecki said driving past the John Fedo Clock Tower at the entrance to Canal Park.

"There!" Callahan yelled. He was looking beyond ICO, pointing with is chin.

Davecki followed the glance. He saw a green flash

vanish between the Dairy Queen and Mobil Station. Davecki jammed second gear. The mighty high compression pistons exherted their best engine braking. This, along with Davecki's foot on the brake pedal, made the Stang slow like a sled dog stopping for hot raw meat. Davecki jerked the steering wheel right. The Mustang fled into the access-way. Davecki floored the foot feed and the car careened around the Dairy Queen drive-through just in time to allow the cops a glimpse of the torpedo shaped car heading into the Meyer-Huff parking lot.

"Go! Go! Go!" Callahan yelled. He pounded the dash.

Davecki drove hard. The Jag drove harder. Together they rocketed south on Lake Avenue toward the aerial lift bridge at over eighty miles-an-hour.

"He's going to Park Point?" Davecki yelled.

"No way," Callahan yelled back.

"He'll go left past DeWitt Seitz. Should I cut him off?"

"What if he goes straight?"

"Thanks for sharing Chief. Now what? Left or pursue?"

"Stay on him!"

The cars sped through the green light at Adventure World. Grandma's Sports Garden whipped past on the right. "He's going over," Davecki yelled as the Jag sped straight over the lift bridge. The Mustang roared as Davecki left the car in third gear. It lofted skyward as they crested the bridge approach. The tires sang as they rolled across the steel mesh deck of the hundred-year old structure. Davecki looked left down the ship canal. Out beyond the lighthouse, the fog was lifting, he could see the prow of a huge ship emerging from the gloom.

"This is nuts!" Davecki yelled as the car exploded out of the end of the bridge tunnel like a potato being shot from a spud gun.

"He's as good as trapped. There's a laker coming in!"

"Unless he's got a boat or something," Callahan said.

"We'd be on him before he could get line one off a cleat," Davecki answered as he shifted to fourth.

"Maybe a plane at Sky Harbor?" The Chief asked.

"He'd never get airborne," Davecki said.

Ahead, the Jaguar's break lights lit up. The car jetted right, vanished down 9th Avenue.

Davecki slowed and followed. He was halfway to the Corp of Engineer's driveway when he realized the truth. "Maybe we're the trapped ones!"

"Huh?" Callahan called.

"If he can get across the bridge before it lifts and we can't, we'll be the ones stuck out here."

"He can't outrun radio frequency," Callahan said holding up his phone.

"He won't have to if he can ditch us long enough to get lost and leave the country."

"DPD will be there,"

"Maybe," Davecki said as he raced his car after the ass-end of the English auto ahead. They careened around Halverson Corner.

Something in the Water

The Jag ripped through the light fog as if visibility was unlimited to fifty miles. Whirls of fog/mist tornadoed behind the aerodynamic car. Then again, brake lights. The car turned left. It sped away.

"He's trying to time the bridge," Davecki yelled.

"He'll never make it. The yellow light was already flashing as we crossed."

Davecki tortured his engine by leaving the car in second and pushing the tachometer needle past the red-line. "If he gets across the bridge before us, he'll be gone."

"I'll shoot his tires out first, if you can get us close enough."

"This isn't a movie, B.D."

The Chief pulled his revolver out anyway. It was an old Dan Wesson heavy frame 357. Four inch barrel. Brown hand grips, wooden. I'm going to plug the bastard. Just get me close!"

Davecki followed the car through the left turn onto Lake Avenue. The Jag sped away. The Mustang started to fall behind.

"Closer!" Callahan yelled.

"We're at top speed now."

"Shit," Callahan said.

"Look!" Davecki said.

Ahead the stop-arm was down blocking traffic. The yellow light had turned red and flashed its warning. A fuchsia Escort wagon sat patiently at the gate. The bridge had not yet started its lift. Navarone swerved around the Escort and smashed through the stop-arm. The bridge deck started up. The Jag ca-

228

reened onto the deck. Brake lights glowed instantly.

Davecki jammed on his brakes. The Mustang skidded around the Escort. As the car careened by on squealing tires, the Escort driver, a blonde woman who looked a lot like a Loon, raised her eyes in surprise. The lurching car screeched to a halt between the broken off stop-arm and the massive bridge deck which was inching slowly upward. Davecki jumped out, and, before sprinting for the lifting bridge, gave the stunned Loon Woman a smart little salute ala Darrel and Darrel on the Bob Newhart show. Callahan also jumped out and followed Davecki who leaped up onto the ascending bridge. The rotound Chief of Police flung himself at the bridge deck and grabbed at the steel mesh decking with the hand that wasn't filled with .357 Magnum. Davecki leaned down and grabbed the Chief's belt. Heaving for all he was worth, Davecki hauled Captain Lunker aboard the sky-bound architecture at the last second.

An alarm was clanging. A synthetic sounding voice blared a warning from unseen speakers, "The bridge is now lifting! The bridge is now lifting! Davecki and Callahan turned from the edge of the bridge deck in time to see Navarone jump out of his Jaguar and dart for the other end of the structure. The metallic voice of the pre-recorded warning stopped in mid-sentence and a real voice blared out of the loud speakers. "Do not approach the end of the bridge. Stay in the center of the span!"

Despite the warning, Navarone kept running. For an old guy he was fast.

Something in the Water

Davecki ran. "He's trying to bail before we get too high," he shouted.

"Halt Police!" Callahan barked as they ran.

Navarone sped up.

"He's going to jump!" Davecki bellowed.

"Stop in the name of the law or I'll shoot!" Callahan yelled.

Davecki looked at Callahan as they chased Navarone, "What?" he shrieked.

Callahan hollered, "Just run asshole!"

Navarone reached the edge of the moving roadway. He paused. He looked back at the pursuing policemen.

"NO!" Callahan yelled.

"STOP!" Davecki yelled.

They could see something Navarone couldn't. The ascending bridge deck was about to glide past one of the main structural beams of the frame of the superstructure. Navarone laughed, turned and leapt without hesitation. Just as his feet left the rising roadway, his head struck the fixed beam. The blow threw Navarone backwards. He grasped for the edge of the bridge deck frantic to pull himself to safety. But it was futile. The rising bridge kept moving like a gigantic paper cutter.

Davecki skidded to a stop. Callahan nearly fell over trying to halt his forward progress. They both stood transfixed. As if in slow motion the two steel edges of the bridge sliced Navarone's seven thousand dollar suit neatly in half. Blood gushed everywhere.

The sight of Navarone's geyser of gore brought

the sight of Thurber Gronsby's corpse to Davecki's mind. He had an instant urge to puke. As his guts tried to heave themselves through his throat, he did what worked for him on Wisconsin Point. He looked lakeward, looked beyond the looming presence of the incoming ship. His urge to vomit passed.

Callahan on the other hand couldn't stop. He went down like Monica Lewinski. He leaned over, held his guts with both hands and barfed six quarts from a four quart stomach. Which is to say, he wretched miserably. After gagging for a minute or more, he gasped and said, "I guess it's true."

"What?" Davecki said holding one hand on his own guts when he saw Navarone's torso twitch.

"The lift bridge **is** like a vegomatic."

"How so,"Davecki asked.

"It slices. It dices," Callahan answered.

Davecki groaned, bent at the waist and puked like a teeny bopper from Cloquet after a quart of Vodka. Now on his hands and knees retching, Davecki looked through the bridge's grated decking and saw Navarone's torrent of blood flushing down the steel beams and into the canal. As sirens approached from downtown, Davecki said, "Plutonium and bodies the lake could take. But this? This is real pollution."

"Huh?" Callahan asked.

Davecki watched as the prow of the Paul A. Delancy glided toward the span they stood on. Davecki stood up. He looked at the Chief and muttered, "I said there's something in the water."

31

Richard "B.D." Callahan's face was locked in a singular, frozen mask of fear.

"Samatter Chief?" Davecki asked.

"I'm afraid of heights," Callahan answered.

"And here I thought the sight of a man sliced in half was bothering you," Davecki said.

"I saw lots worse in Nam and I puked then too," Callahan said.

Then they heard another sound, the sound of a car door opening. They turned toward Superior and saw that the Jaguar door had been opened. They saw a pair of shapely legs reaching out of the rider's door frame onto the bridge deck. From behind the tinted glass a woman's figure emerged. It was Sparky Anderson.

Davecki touched the Chief's shoulder and started walking toward the hooker. The Chief stayed put, clutching a guard rail with both meaty fists. As Davecki walked, the long, long deck of the Delancy flowed past below his feet like a silent-giant steel-eel. The fog was lifting all across the harbor. For the first time, Davecki noticed the resounding blast of *Toot The Hoot*, the old diaphanous fog horn. Its bellow kept the cake eaters of east Duluth awake nights and exposed the city to serious litigation by a whole class of angry citizens. Disregarding *Toot*, Davecki realized the view from the uplifting bridge was not only inspiring, it was spectacular. Duluth could make a lot of money if it reinstituted bridge rides, Davecki thought. The curvature of the earth was evident to the east as he looked out across the broad waters of Mother Superior. Barges dotted the middle distance marking the barrel dumping sites. The Delancy's white superstructure was approaching. Down on the piers, the gathering crowd looked like ants clustering around a sugar cube.

"I'm glad he's dead," Sparky said as Davecki walked up. The hooker waved toward the many-windowed flat front of the big ship's white face as it drew closer. Several people were gathered at the large picture window that was on the right side of the flagship of the fleet's superstructure. They were guests of the fleet who had just cruised up from Cleveland or some such port. The kids in the window waved back. The adults were looking wildly at the crowd, at the bridge and at the people on the bridge.

The Captain who was on the starboard flying bridge watching his ship's progress through the narrow canal was pointing to the pair of legs and obscene streak of blood and gore on the approach apron of the bridge. Far below, women were screaming.

"Everybody's gotta go sometime," Davecki said. He held his breath as the blast of Bunker C exhaust from the twin stacks of the 13,000 horsepower engines passed below. Sparky's lime green skirt flew up like she was Norma Jean on a sidewalk grate. "What happened?" Davecki asked.

"About an hour ago he came over and asked if I wanted to go to Rio with him. I asked him for how long and he said, 'I'm going forever.'"

Something in the Water

They walked to the west edge of the bridge. The big ship's nose was a thousand feet into its graceful left turn into the harbor. Twin trails of turbulent water roiled behind the stern of the massive motor vessel. Davecki leaned onto the guard rail and hooked his elbows over the top cable. He could see the ugly gashes of Spirit Mountain in the distant foliage. He wondered why the eco-extremists didn't bitch about that clear-cut. Maybe the "creepy little jobs" the ski hill created were worth something after all. Sparky faced east. She leaned over the cable, spoke to the lake, "He told me it came to him in a dream. It came to him that his cum would connect him to Hoffa's murder and that, nowhere, really, was safe. So he was leaving the country to try and live happily until they found him."

"They?" Davecki said watching the Delancy glide silently, elegantly into the harbor.

Anderson tossed her hair. "He said the cops or the mob would get him for killing Hoffa. He said nobody could prove he had Gronsby wrapped in a gill net and tossed overboard," she explained.

"So you were going along for the ride?"

"Sure. I ain't done nothing wrong and I never been to Rio. It sounded exciting."

"I'm sure it would have been." Davecki said. The bridge shook as it began its downward trek. "You'll get your quota of excitement explaining all this to the cops and media. In the meantime, I'm hungry. I'm going to the Anchor. Wanna come?" he said turning around to face The Great Lake.

Anderson looked at Davecki. She grinned and said, "I never come. But I'll go. I'm hungry too."

Sunlight reflected off the Big Sea Shining Waters like a quadrillion diamonds were floating across the entire surface of the Jewel of America. The two stared at the Living Waters.

"God that's beautiful," Anderson said.

"There sure is something about that water," Davecki agreed.

"I'm glad Thurber saved it," Anderson said.

"I think it saved itself," Davecki answered.

THE END

About the Author

 Mike Savage was born in Ashland, Wisconsin. He did his time as a kid in both Iron River, and Cornucopia, Wisconsin. From these days he excavated two books, *Growing Up Wild in Wisconsin* and *Raised by Savages*. Following his education at the South Shore School District he attended the University of Wisconsin at Superior where he took a class in Medieval Literature from Professor David Light whose delight in literature and brilliant teaching methods inspired the youth's interest in writing. Following several years of job hopping that included stints as a tent revival worker, a salad chef, short order cook, disc jockey, auto-mechanic, and logger, a catastrophic traffic accident ended his logging business and launched a writing binge. He sold over 1,000 articles and many more photos to such publications as; <u>Reader's Digest</u>, <u>The Covenant Companion</u>, <u>Power for Living</u>, the <u>Superior Evening Telegram</u>, the <u>St. Louis Post-Dispatch</u>, the <u>Milwaukee Sentinel</u>, the <u>Milwaukee Journal</u>, <u>St. Paul Pioneer Press-Dispatch</u>, <u>Alaska Business Monthly</u>, <u>Nome Nugget</u>, the <u>Timber Producer</u>, <u>Timber Harvesting</u>, <u>Farmer Magazine,</u> and many others. He became a corresponding editor for Hatton-Brown Publications of Montgomery, Alabama. In 1989 he started Savage Press publishing *The Northern Reader*, and the book, *Stop in the Name of the Law*. Since then Savage Press has published 45 books the latest of which is *Something in the Water*.

Photo by Mary Brooks

Other Books Available from Savage Press

Hometown Wisconsin by Marshall J. Cook

Treasures from the Beginning of the World by Jeff Lewis

Stop in the Name of the Law by Alex O'Kash

A Hint of Frost — Essays from the Earth by Rusty King

Widow of the Waves by Bev Jamison

Appalachian Mettle by Paul Bennett

Gleanings from the Hillsides by E.M. Johnson

Poems of Faith and Inspiration by E.M. Johnson

Keeper of the Town by Don Cameron

Thicker Than Water by Hazel Sangster

Moments Beautiful Moments Bright by Brett Bartholomaus

Some Things You Never Forget by Clem Miller

The Year of the Buffalo,
a novel of love and minor league baseball
by Marshall J. Cook

Pathways by Mary B. Wadzinski

Superior Catholics by Cheney & Meronek

Beyond the Mine, a Steelworker's Story by Peter J. Benzoni

Jackpine Savages by Frank Larson

The Duluth Tour Book by Jeff Cornelius

SoundBites:
A Business Guide to Working with the Media
by Kathy Kerchner

Widow of the Waves by Bev Jamison

Walker's in the Mist by Hollis D'Normand

Voices from the North Edge by St. Croix Writers

To order additional copies of

Something in the Water

call:

1-800-732-3867

Visa or MasterCard accepted.

To receive a copy of the complete
Savage Press catalog,
contact us at:

Voice and Fax:

(715) 394-9513

e-mail:

savpress@spacestar.com

Web Page:

www.spacestar.net/users/savpress

Box 115, Superior, WI 54880 (715) 394-9513